BOOK
1

PERFECT VILLAINS

JENNIFER TORRES

Scholastic Inc.

This book is a work of fiction. Names, characters, places, and incidents are either the product of the author's imagination or are used fictitiously, and any resemblance to actual persons, living or dead, business establishments, events, or locales is entirely coincidental.

ISBN 978-1-338-83314-0

10 9 8 7 6 5 4 3 2 1   23 24 25 26 27

Printed in the U.S.A.   40
First printing 2023

Book design by Maeve Norton

For Soledad

CHAPTER 1

It is a glittery-golden morning on the first day of school for royalty in training.

Ghastly golden, if you ask Princesa Dominga. She grimaces at the parade of princesas that jostle past her, jewel-toned traveling cloaks billowing over their shoulders as they hurry toward the grand arched entry to the palace.

Dominga tightens her own cloak around her

neck, as though she could make herself disappear behind its black velvet folds. Already, the Fine and Ancient Institute for the Royal is far worse than she ever could have predicted. She should have jumped from her mother's carriage the moment she realized where it was taking her.

She squints into the dazzling sun and wishes she were someplace dark. Someplace dank. Someplace *else*. She closes her eyes and imagines it. She can almost smell the mold and mildew. She can nearly hear the steady *drip drip drip* of sludge down a dungeon wall.

But as soon as she opens her eyes, the scene dissolves. Faster than a nightmare at daybreak.

There is no escape. The last carriages clatter away after late-arriving princesas have said their goodbyes, and the gates clang shut behind them. Dominga's mamá stayed only long enough leave her with a warning: "If I hear any more of this villain nonsense, I'll yank you back to the castle, where you'll spend your days managing Paloma's correspondence." Princesa Paloma—more like *Princesa Perfecta*—is Dominga's older sister. She graduated from the F.A.I.R. the year before and would one day be queen.

If there is anything more appalling than the F.A.I.R., it is the thought of being stuck at home, writing Paloma's letters. Would she have to sign them with the same flourish of hearts and flowers that her sister did? Better to never find out.

Dominga supposes she is stuck. For now. She looks past the locked gate where, no more than a day's walk away, the Bewitched Academy for the Dreadful is perched atop a grim and craggy cliff. Storm clouds as dark as shadows swirl around its spindly towers.

That *is where I should be*, Dominga thinks. That *is where I belong*.

Instead she is here, where blushing blossoms sail on a sweet silken breeze.

"Sickeningly sweet," Dominga mutters, plopping herself down on her trunk to let the swarm of princesas surge ahead without her. A pale pink petal lands on her nose. She sneezes.

"¡Salud!" a voice sings out, even though Dominga is perfectly healthy. "And perhaps next time you can try to sneeze a bit more quietly. I'm *certain* you wouldn't want to cause a commotion, not on the very first day."

Dominga looks up. Standing next to her is a tall girl with coppery-red hair and a yellow gown so bright it almost glows. The girl dips into a deep curtsy. "I am Princesa Inés," she says. "Encantada."

Dominga could not be any less enchanted. She nods back anyway. "Dominga."

"Dominga?" Inés echoes. She gapes at Dominga, from her scuffed black boots to her gold-rimmed glasses. The wrinkled-nose look on Inés's face is a mixture of confusion and disappointment. Dominga has seen this look before.

"As in Princesa Paloma's sister?"

Dominga nods again.

"Paloma was last year's Fairest of the F.A.I.R., you know," Inés continues.

Dominga knows. She could not unknow it if she tried.

A new look crosses Inés's face. Her amber-brown eyes gleam. "In that case," she says, pulling Dominga up by the elbow, "I am *certain* we are going to be friends. *Best* friends. Let's find a spot near the front. No one will notice us all the way back here."

Yes, that is the point, Dominga thinks. She steps back on her heels. "Thank you, but I would prefer to stay—" she protests.

"Nonsense." Inés yanks even harder. Dominga has no choice but to follow, dragging her trunk behind her across the lush green lawn. She casts one last glance at the B.A.D. and its towers that now seem as far away as they've ever been.

Inés catches the look. "Ugh," she says. "I know. Isn't it absolutely *shocking* that we can see that horrid place from here? They should build a higher wall or plant taller trees so we don't have to look at it. In the meantime, we'll just pretend it isn't there, won't we?"

She tilts her chin so high in the air that Dominga wonders how she can tell where she's walking.

"And don't worry," Inés continues. "I'm sure

you'll have time to change out of your—" She turns briefly and wrinkles her nose again. "Traveling clothes."

Dominga looks down at her gown. The top is black, with a spray of crow's feathers at each shoulder. (She collected them herself.) The skirt is midnight blue with silver bats embroidered along its edge.

By the time Dominga looks up again, she realizes that Inés has squeezed and shoved her way to the front of the crowd.

"We're here!" Inés squeals. "And right on time!" The palace doors creak open. Silence ripples across the courtyard. Princesas watch in awe as a short woman with a long, slender nose emerges. She wears a satin vest that shimmers green and lavender. She stands beneath the palace's gilt arches and straightens her neck.

Inés nudges Dominga with her shoulder. "Shh," she shushes, even though Dominga hasn't said anything. "It's all starting. Can you even stand it?"

Dominga cannot.

CHAPTER 2

The woman with the long thin nose flicks open a fan and flutters it so quickly that a wisp of indigo hair blows out of her tidy braided bun.

"Buenos días, princesas."

All together, the princesas curtsy. Their gowns—in soft violet and vibrant marigold, bold scarlet and delicate seafoam—puff up under them so that it looks to Dominga as if a field of rainbow-colored mushrooms has sprouted in front of the palace. Inés takes hold of Dominga's elbow and pulls. "Down," she growls.

"My name is Profesora Colibrí," the woman warbles as they rise. "Welcome to the Fine and Ancient Institute for the Royal."

A wasp hovers near Inés's right ear. Dominga does not mention it.

"While you are here, you will grow in courage and creativity," Profesora Colibrí continues. "Friendship and fondness for knowledge."

The wasp flies even closer. Dominga does not flick it away.

"But before we begin, we must assign each of you to a Casita: Ruby, Emerald, Sapphire, or Opal."

Inés recites the names along with her. *Perhaps the wasp will fly into her mouth*, Dominga thinks. *Since it's always open and all.*

"Your Casita will be your home—your

family—during your time here," Profesora Colibrí says. "Do not be discouraged if the cottage you are assigned is not the one you expected. You may discover it is exactly where you belong."

Dominga doubts it. But she has prepared for this moment ever since Paloma described it in one of her letters home. She wrote *so* many letters. Paloma had been assigned to Casita Opal. No one was surprised, least of all Mamá. The Fairest of the F.A.I.R. was *always* an Opal princesa, and they had *always* known that Paloma was destined to be the Fairest of the F.A.I.R.

"When you enter the Great Hall, you will see four chalices, one representing each Casita," Profesora Colibrí says. "Every noble deed will earn your Casita a gem. The cottage with the most gems in their cup at the end of the term will be declared Fairly Royal—"

The princesas clap, Inés loudest of all. Dominga drops back onto her trunk.

"—and," Profesora Colibrí continues, "earn the privilege of venturing off the palace grounds and into the village as ambassadors of the F.A.I.R."

Dominga jumps to her feet. *Off the palace grounds?* Why had Paloma never mentioned *that?* Then again, maybe she had. Dominga tended to drift into daydreams when Mamá read Paloma's letters aloud over breakfast. Paloma's letters were always so long. Now thoughts of escape whir through Dominga's mind.

"Let's get started," Profesora Colibrí announces. "Princesas, if you please, form an orderly line."

Faster than Dominga would have imagined possible—and just as the wasp was about to alight on her ear—Inés leaps ahead and lands first in line.

She smooths her lemony skirt and pulls her

satin gloves up over her elbows. "Encantada." She curtsies. "I am Princesa Inés, and I am ready, Profesora."

Profesora Colibrí peers down her nose at Inés. "Opal," she declares without hesitation. She flutters her fan over Inés's head. A tiara appears out of a swirl of smoke and sparkle and slowly falls onto her copper curls. It is a gold circlet of leaves and flowers, their petals fashioned out of glowing opals with crystals at their centers.

The other princesas gasp. Dominga swallows a groan. It's a nice enough tiara, but it's not like they've never seen one before.

Inés twirls before lifting her trunk by its handle and setting off down the lily-lined path to the Casitas.

Dominga fights the urge to bolt. Then she takes a breath and pats her pocket. It's still there, the thing she is counting on to get her out of this predicament. The line steps forward, and Dominga moves along with it.

When it's finally her turn, Dominga stands before Profesora Colibrí, twisting the black ribbons that fasten her cloak. "Hello," she says. "It's me. Dominga."

Profesora Colibrí tilts her head. "Ah, Princesa Dominga," she says. "You have your sister's . . ." She stops. She considers. "Your sister's . . . eyebrows," she says after a pause. "And, like Paloma, you will join Casita Opal." She lifts her arm, preparing to wave her fan.

"W-wait!" Dominga says, her voice catching. "Actually, I . . . um . . . I would like to suggest a new Casita." She reaches into her pocket and pulls out a smooth black stone. "Obsidian." She says the word slowly. "It comes from *volcanoes*." She could almost stand to wear a tiara if it were made of stones like this. She could almost bear to be here if she had a place to belong.

The princesses in line go very quiet. Dominga hears their skirts rustle as they shuffle forward to listen. She tries not to think about their eyes fixed on the back of her head—or about what Mamá would say if she heard what Dominga had asked.

Profesora Colibrí lowers her arm. She takes a stumbling step backward, almost tripping on her skirt with its colors that seem to shift in the light. "Obsidian?" she repeats. "How . . . *different.* I've never heard of . . ." She fans her face, mouth opening and closing. Finally, she shakes her head. "No. Opal, I think. Filled with fire and mystery." She lifts her arm again and flutters her fan.

Dominga looks up just as a silver tiara with

clusters of round opals like fizz in a potion bottle settles onto her head.

It already pinches.

"Next," the profesora calls.

Dominga's last hope has burst in a cloud of smoke and sparkle. She doesn't move. She can't. She doesn't know where to go from here.

After several long moments, she feels a light tap on her shoulder, not unlike the beating of a bat wing.

"Huh?" She spins around. The next princesa in line lifts both eyebrows at Dominga. With her chin, she gestures toward the path that leads to the Casitas. "You can go now," she whispers.

"Oh," Dominga says. "Of course." She drops her piece of obsidian, its shine a little duller, into her pocket. She lifts her trunk and drags it to the path.

She lingers there, watching as the rest of the

princesas are assigned to their Casitas. Some are Emeralds, some are Rubies, some are Sapphires. A few more are Opals, but none are like Dominga.

She might as well find her room. She is about to head down the path when she notices the last princesa in line.

The girl is tucking a lizard into the pocket of her swampy-green gown.

"No pets in the palace, Princesa Dalia," Profesora Colibrí scolds. "As I have already told you and your grandparents. On more than one occasion."

Dalia cups the lizard in her hands and holds it out to Profesora Colibrí. "But he's very well-behaved, Profesora," she pleads. "You won't even know he's here."

Profesora Colibrí snaps her fan shut and presses her lips together.

"Oh, all right," Dalia relents. She kneels,

whispers something to the lizard, and releases it into a row of purple geraniums.

Dominga pats her pocket. At least Profesora Colibrí didn't make her give up the stone.

"Now, then," the profesora says. She squints down at Dalia. "Emerald, obviously. A symbol of loyalty and *fresh starts*." She flicks her fan, and the tiara lands crookedly on Dalia's head. "Go and find your place, Princesa."

At that, Dominga turns and hurries down the path. She doesn't want Dalia to know she's been spying. But she peeks back once more, in time to see Profesora Colibrí return to the palace with a swish of her skirts. Once she is inside, Dalia taps her toe on the cobblestones. The lizard scurries out of the flowers and crawls into her boot.

Perhaps, Dominga thinks, quickening her pace, *there is something different about Dalia.*

CHAPTER
3

After a breakfast of pastelitos and pan dulce the next morning, Dominga wonders whether the palace baker uses homemade butter. She thinks he probably does. Not that she enjoyed the pastries *very* much.

She gathers with the rest of the princesas in a forest clearing at the edge of the palace grounds. They had followed Profesora Colibrí through a dense, dark forest of pines and ancient oaks to get here, their shoes squishing into a thick blanket of leaves and toadstools.

Dominga touches her tiara. Earlier that morning, Inés insisted on securing it with hairpins, seven of them, to keep it from falling off.

"Quiet!" Inés barks now, stepping up beside her. "Woodland Wildlife class is about to begin. And we don't want Opal to lose any gems." She narrows her sparkling amber eyes. *"Do we?"*

Dominga shakes her head and takes a small, wary step away.

At the center of the clearing is a crystal-blue pond, surrounded by swaying cattails. Profesora Colibrí stands among them, her fan all aflutter.

"Remember, princesas," she explains, "everything in the forest is connected. Each creature, even the smallest, has an important part to play."

Dominga yawns.

Inés stomps on her toe.

"¡Ay!" Dominga squeals, then thinks, *I should have stepped farther away.*

"Oops," Inés whispers, smiling sweetly. "I thought I saw a centipede. I wouldn't want it to crawl up your boot."

"I wouldn't have minded," Dominga mutters.

"What was that?" Inés raises her hands to her hips.

"Nothing."

Profesora Colibrí continues. "Today you will explore the woodland habitat. Investigate! Discover! Be prepared to tell us what you learn from the wild things all around you. The Fairest of the F.A.I.R. must be in tune with the rhythms of nature. She must speak the language of the forest. The princesa with the most inspiring presentation will earn ten gems for her Casita's chalice."

The other princesas cheer.

Dominga claps absently. Each of those gems could bring her closer to escape. But this morning she has another mission in mind.

She must observe Dalia. She must find out if her suspicions are correct.

The class scatters across the clearing, and Dominga follows the Emerald princesas into the meadow that surrounds the pond. One of them spots a robin hopping on the ground, searching for insects. The princesas form a wide circle around the bird and mimic its whistle. *Cheer-up! Cheerily cheer-up!*

"Brilliant birdcalls!" Profesora Colibrí applauds. The princesas continue chirping.

But not Dalia. Dalia sneaks into the shadows and starts hissing. Dominga could be wrong, but it sounds exactly like a turkey vulture.

Dominga creeps closer. Slowly, staying close to

the trees, she reaches into her pocket and takes out her spell book. It has a red leather cover and gold-edged pages and was a gift from Paloma. Of course, it hadn't always been a spell book.

"A diary!" Paloma had said, passing it to Dominga through the carriage window on the morning of her departure. "So you won't forget a single moment." Inside, she had written her top three Rules for Royalty:

- A true princesa makes the most of every situation.
- A true princesa always presents her most splendid self.
- A true princesa never loses her way.

She had even drawn a map of the palace. "It's quite easy to get lost at the F.A.I.R."

Dominga pulls a pencil from her tangled brown bun, flips past Paloma's map, and opens the book to an empty page.

Observations, she scrawls on top.

Knows beastly birdcalls, she writes underneath.

"There you are!"

Dominga startles and looks behind her. It is Inés. The opals in her tiara flicker like candle flames. Dominga slams her spell book shut.

"What's that?" Inés asks. "This is no time for scribbling. You should be helping Casita Opal search for animal tracks so we can win this challenge."

Dominga points to the robin in the meadow. "In fact, I was just—"

"Never mind," Inés interrupts. "You don't need to apologize. Just follow me."

Dominga sticks the pencil back in her bun. She

drops the spell book in her pocket and trudges behind Inés, eyes on the ground.

That's where she finds a solution.

"There!" Dominga shouts. She points to the dirt, where the boots of dozens of princesas have left a smattering of small dents. "Hoofprints," she says. "Deer, I think."

Inés's shimmering hair whips into Dominga's face as she swivels her head. "Tracks?" She peers at the ground, then waves over the rest of the Opal princesas.

"I've found deer tracks," she tells them, pointing with the toe of her chalk-white slipper. "And they're fresh."

Princesa Pilar bends low to the ground. "They look too small to be deer."

"They might be . . . *baby* deer?" Dominga suggests, avoiding Pilar's eyes.

"That's what I said. *Baby* deer. Obviously," Inés replies with a huff. "We should follow these tracks. A fawn might need my help." She takes off running into the meadow, her yellow skirt skimming the grass.

The other princesas gallop after her.

"Bravo!" Profesora Colibrí calls. "Caring for small creatures is our royal responsibility."

Dominga slips away from the crowd without Inés noticing. She crouches beside a blackberry bramble, thorny and wild, and wishes there were someone nearby to congratulate her for the ruse. But villains, she knows, rarely get the credit they deserve.

Besides, there is little time to waste. She looks for Dalia where she last saw her, in the shadows under the pine trees. But she is no longer there. With a shiver of worry, Dominga wonders if she followed the others, chasing after hoofprints that are not really hoofprints toward a fawn that doesn't exist. Impossible. Not if Dalia is who Dominga thinks she is.

Then again, maybe she isn't.

Leaves rustle on the other side of the blackberry bush. Dominga peers over, and there is Dalia. Tracking the zigzagging trail of a rat snake.

Dominga steps out from behind the bramble. She has always wanted to inspect a snake den.

But she stops herself. It is too soon. She must gather more evidence. She must be certain. So she crouches again behind the bramble and opens her spell book to the page of observations. *Can identify snake tra—* she begins to write.

Before she can finish, she hears a frantic squeal. "They're hungry!" someone yells.

Dominga's head snaps up. Perhaps forest

predators are on the hunt! Perhaps a flock of angry robins has swooped down from their branches to quiet the chattering princesas. Perhaps this class is not so very dull after all.

But of course, that cannot be true.

Dominga realizes the commotion is only some chipmunks nibbling out of the hands of the Sapphire princesas.

"We're going to need more acorns!" Princesa Jacinta shouts.

The princesas race toward the oak trees. Dalia does not seem to notice. She is too busy with the bullfrogs that have gathered at her feet. She kneels and croaks and pats their slimy heads.

Yes, Dominga decides. *There seems to be something different about Dalia.*

Dreadfully different. Dominga can tell because *she* is dreadful too.

But now, at last, there is only one way to be certain. Dominga has been careful not to reveal herself to anyone since she arrived. What would the princesas do if they discovered there was a villain in their midst? Probably snitch to Profesora Colibrí. Who would probably call her mamá, who would *definitely* return from her royal realm to take Dominga back home, where the B.A.D. would be forever out of reach.

And yet, she decides she must take the risk. Dominga is not yet a powerful enough villain to escape these princesas on her own. She can barely avoid Inés.

If she had a partner, though, they could make some mischief. They could hatch some schemes. They could take over the castle! They could escape to the B.A.D.!

But she is getting ahead of herself.

Dominga closes her eyes and takes a deep breath. When she opens her eyes, she sees Dalia at the edge of the pond, digging in the dirt with the tip of a wooden wand.

Probably hunting for earthworms. Probably to feed the bullfrogs. The edge of her skirt is caked with mud, and a spider weaves its web in her tiara.

Dominga pushes her glasses up the bridge of her nose. She wishes she knew a magic spell for courage. She doesn't, though, and she can't put this off any longer.

CHAPTER 4

When she has tiptoed as close to Dalia as she dares, Dominga squawks. "Skreek!" She flaps her arms and scratches her toes in the ground.

Arms still outstretched, Dominga's eyes dart right and left, checking to see whether any of the other princesas are watching. Her cheeks go warm just thinking about it. "Skreek!" she squawks again. She wishes she'd had more time to practice at home, that she'd had someone to practice *with*. Still, she is confident this is decent enough turkey vulture for "Excuse me, but I don't think you belong here."

Only someone *dreadfully* good at awful animal sounds would understand. Someone like Dominga.

And maybe, if Dominga is lucky, someone like Dalia too. But so far, Dalia has not even raised her eyes. It's as if she doesn't notice her at all.

Dominga takes another step closer. "Skreek?" she says again, more quietly this time.

Finally, Dalia drops her wand and peers out from behind her dark curls. She blinks back at Dominga. She says nothing.

Then she scowls.

Dominga cringes. She skitters backward and reaches to tighten the ribbons on her cloak before remembering she isn't wearing one. It seems Dalia doesn't understand her after all. No one does.

No matter, Dominga tells herself. *Who ever heard of a villain making friends, anyway?* She tries to swallow down a lump of disappointment, but it seems to be stuck at the back of her throat.

She is about to retreat to her hiding place behind the blackberry bush when Dalia swipes the hair out of her eyes and clears her throat.

Dominga stops. She listens.

"Tuk tuk tuk," Dalia says then. It is impeccable turkey vulture, much better than Dominga's, for "Well, to be honest, I don't think you belong here either."

Dominga is pretty sure she knows what she heard, but doesn't quite believe it. "Would you mind repeating that?" she asks.

Dalia sits back on her heels. "You heard me."

Glee burbles inside Dominga like bubbles in a boiling cauldron. When she can no longer contain it, she leaps, kicking up a clod of dirt with the pointy toe of her boot. "Eeek!"

"Bravo!"

Huh? Dalia and Dominga twist their necks around.

It is Profesora Colibrí, striding toward them, her fan fluttering faster than ever. "Princesas, you have perfected the noble call of the turkey vulture," she says, patting Dominga on the shoulder. "And on only the second day."

They have been caught. They will need to be more careful from now on. More *cunning*.

"Gracias, Profesora," Dominga manages to reply. "We'll keep practicing." Profesora Colibrí flicks her fan shut as she saunters toward the Sapphire princesses who are now climbing an oak tree.

"Notice the life in its branches!" she calls. "Insects! Birds! Moss!"

Dominga lowers her voice and leans forward. "You're Dalia, right?" she says. "I'm Dominga. And, maybe, we don't belong . . . *together*. Maybe we are the *same* kind of different."

Dalia croaks at the bullfrogs. They hop aside, and Dalia points at the now empty space next to her. "Would you like to sit?"

Dominga freezes for a moment. It's not only that the frogs seemed to have obeyed Dalia. It's that no one has invited her to sit down with them before. "I think I would," she says, hoping she sounds as if it happens all the time.

She drops to the soft, squelchy ground beside Dalia. A frog splashes into the mud between them, leaving Dominga spattered with sludge. Dalia takes a handkerchief from the inside of her puffed green sleeve and offers it to her.

"Did you know," Dalia says as Dominga wipes her glasses, "that rhinoceroses often cover themselves in mud? On *purpose*? It's to protect their skin from the sun."

Dominga returns the handkerchief and looks out at the other students in the clearing. "It *is* a terribly sunny day," she observes.

Dalia removes her gloves and scoops up a glob of goo with her bare hand. "Are you suggesting a mud bath?" she asks. "To protect the princesas from sunburn?"

Dominga cackles. She can already picture it. But she shakes her head. They still have important business to discuss. The *most* important business.

"Perhaps later," she says.

Dalia shrugs and dribbles the mud over the

bullfrogs. She wipes her hands on her skirt. "Then what do you suggest?"

Dominga must be sure no one is listening. She looks right. Princesas from Casita Emerald are still chasing robins across the meadow. She looks left. Princesas from Casita Ruby are steps away, inspecting a beaver's dam.

She turns back to Dalia. In a whisper she asks, "Have you ever heard of . . ." She stops. She swallows. She glances around again. "The Bewitched Academy for the Dreadful?"

Dalia blows the curls out of her face. "Do you mean the school for the cruelest villains, the rottenest rascals, and the dirtiest tricksters? The one that's right over those hills, no more than a day's walk from here?"

"I knew it!" Dominga squeals. Profesora Colibrí,

standing at the base of the largest oak tree, turns. "Princesas?"

Dominga opens her mouth to explain, but no words come out.

"Dominga is practicing the call of the Southern Screamer," Dalia yells. Satisfied, Profesora Colibrí flutters her fan and peers into the branches.

Dominga should have thought of that. She lowers her voice. "Thank you. As I was saying, you *have* heard of it."

The first time Dominga spied the ravens circling the soaring stone towers of the B.A.D. was through the window of Mamá's carriage. Paloma had started school that fall, and they were on their way for a visit. Dominga has known since that day that it is the only place she can learn to become the villain she is truly meant to be.

Mamá refused to even let her apply.

But perhaps there is still hope. Perhaps she can get there on her own. Perhaps she and Dalia can get there together.

"Of course I have heard of the B.A.D.," Dalia answers. "Any villain who can cast the most basic itching curse has." She frowns. "But we'll never get out of here. And even if we did, they will never give us a place. Not unless we prove we are definitely dreadful."

It's true, Dominga knows. The B.A.D. is notoriously selective.

A squeal from the meadow distracts them. The Emerald princesas are helping a blackbird fill her nest with bits of fluff. It is horribly adorable.

"What this place needs is something awful," Dalia complains.

"Something ghastly," Dominga agrees.

But there is nothing even close.

Except, of course, the two of them.

Dominga sits up taller. "Perhaps," she says, "if we work together, we can think of something dreadful. Something the B.A.D. cannot possibly ignore."

CHAPTER 5

Dominga gazes out across the sparkling pond. Dragonflies flit over the white and pink water lilies that bob on its surface. Small turtles with red stripes on their cheeks sun themselves on the rocks before sliding into the water. The Ruby princesas, skirts hitched to their knees, wade in with nets.

"But how will we do that here?" Dalia asks.

"Suppose we fill the pond with piranhas,"

Dominga proposes. She imagines the screams of frantic princesas—the buzzing swarm of dragonflies, the scuffle of turtle feet—as they all flee a school of chomping fish with knife-sharp teeth. She rubs her hands together in villainous anticipation.

Dalia shakes her head. She swipes away a curl that has fallen into her face. "Piranhas rarely attack unless threatened," she explains with the same bored patience as one of Dominga's old tutors. "It is a common misconception."

Dominga looks away. She should have known that. *Should* she have known that? Do *all* villains know that? They've met only minutes ago and already Dalia will think she is terrifically unprepared.

"Not piranhas," Dominga agrees, voice shaky. "Of course. How could I forget?" She throws herself backward onto the soggy ground and stares up into the trees.

One of the robins settles on a leafy branch, lifts its head, and trills. *The princesas seem to be distracted by that nest*, it says.

Finally, another one chirps back. *We can hunt our worms in peace.*

Dominga sits up. "We're both terribly good at birdcalls, aren't we?"

"I've been teaching myself for the past four years," Dalia says.

Four years? That's far longer than Dominga has been practicing. She doesn't admit it. "Right," she continues. "Well, suppose we mimic a robin's warning call. Convince every bird in the forest that a hawk is near."

Birds would fly from their nests, screeching and screaming. Hundreds of birds. No, *thousands!*

Dominga jumps to her feet, already picturing the chaos. "Think of the noise!" she shouts. "Think of the *mess*!"

Dalia tugs the edge of her skirt to pull her back to the ground. Too late, Dominga realizes she has gotten ahead of herself again. Princesa Inés skips toward them, coppery ringlets bouncing under her tiara.

"There you are," Inés says, hands on her hips. "We've been looking all over. Why aren't you helping us find the fawn?" She wrinkles her nose at Dalia. "Why are you with *her*? And what's happened to your gown?"

So many questions. Dominga scrambles to come up with an answer to any of them. An answer that will not get her and Dalia caught before they have had the chance to do *anything* very dreadful. But Inés's unblinking glare makes it impossible to think clearly.

"We are cooking up a plot!" she blurts. She slaps her hand over her mouth, immediately realizing her mistake.

"What Dominga means is," Dalia says, standing, "we are coming up with a *plan*. Something special for Profesora Colibrí—for the whole class, really."

It is the truth, and yet not. Dominga watches with wonder and . . . something else. Something that should be admiration, but isn't. Something that prickles.

Inés opens her mouth as if she is about to argue. But then she stops. She takes one hand off her hip to scratch her nose. "Cooperation," she says. "Clever. Profesora Colibrí might even award extra gems for working together. So what's the plan? You'll need my help, of course."

Help from Inés is the last thing they need. "But that would spoil the scheme . . . I mean, the *surprise*," Dominga argues.

Inés looks from Dalia to Dominga. "I love a surprise," she says.

Just then, another princesa calls out to her from the forest path. "Inés! We think it went this way!"

"Wait for me," Inés calls back.

Dominga sneaks a glance at Dalia. Her widening eyes say, *That was a close one, but I think she's leaving.*

Dalia blinks back as if to agree. *It's about time. I thought we'd never get rid of her.*

"I'd better go. My team needs me," Inés says, stepping closer to Dominga. "Keep working on

that surprise. And *don't*. Mess. Up." She punctu-
ates each word with a stomp of her foot, then
smiles and curtsies and skips away.

Dalia sinks back down to the ground.

"So," Dominga says, sitting next to her, "what
do you think? About the robins, I mean."

Dalia picks up one of the bullfrogs and sets it
on her lap. She dangles an earthworm over its
head. The frog leaps up and swallows it.

"Robins are difficult to trick," she says after
a while. "They'll never believe it. A squirrel,
maybe—they love to make deals—but we have
nothing to trade." Two more bullfrogs hop toward
her, and she tosses each of them a worm.

Dominga picks up a rock and hurls it at the
water. It skips twice, then sinks. "It's worth a try,
at least," she grumbles. "What makes you think

you know so much about wild animals, anyway?" This is turning out to be almost like having
another Princesa Perfecta around.

"I've spent a lot of time with animals," Dalia
replies. Her voice is so quiet Dominga can hardly
hear her, especially over the bullfrogs. "Animals
make very good friends when . . . when you don't
have anyone else to talk to." Her curls fall over her
face again. She doesn't brush them away this time.

"Oh," Dominga says. "Oh."

Dalia feeds the last worm to the smallest frog,
then croaks gently at the others. They hop into the
reeds, leaving the pond suddenly still. "On second
thought," she says after a while, "you're right."

"I *am*?" Princesa Perfecta would never have
said *that*. "What do you mean?"

"I mean," Dalia says, "it's worth a try."

CHAPTER
6

Dalia twists her hair into a knot and pokes her wand through to secure it. She sits with her legs folded underneath her and stares at Dominga.

Dominga stares back until she realizes, with a jittery mix of surprise and excitement, that Dalia is waiting for her to say what they should do next.

"Oh!" She fumbles in her pocket for the spell

book to give herself a few more moments to think. She opens to a blank page and pulls out her pencil.

Wicked Schemes, she writes on top.

Below that, she draws a small black dot and next to it writes *Robin Ruckus*. She taps the pencil against the page. "I suppose," she says, "we should practice first."

The trouble is, Dominga has only ever practiced birdcalls in her room with all the windows shut tight so that Mamá doesn't hear. She's never tried them out on real birds before, let alone in front of someone else.

Dalia leans over to read Dominga's notes. "We'll have to make it sound *real*, like there is actual danger nearby," she says. "That's the only way to fool a robin." Dominga scribbles down every word, hoping Dalia will keep talking.

"It helps if you imagine something frightening

first—the most dangerous thing you can think of," Dalia goes on. "Like this."

Dalia squeezes her eyes shut. Her jaw clenches and her forehead wrinkles. Dominga wonders what terrible image she is bringing to mind.

Then Dalia's eyes pop open and she whistles, high and shrill. Dominga covers her ears and pushes herself backward. When Dalia's breath runs out and her whistle sputters to silence, the two of them turn toward the oak.

A furious chatter rises from the branches.

What's that? the birds twitter back. *What's going on?*

Princesa Jacinta, who has climbed halfway up the trunk, looks warily into the leaves.

"Now you try," Dalia says.

Spell book resting in her lap, Dominga closes her eyes.

She imagines being fitted for a sparkling new gown like Inés's, the crinkly fabric pulled tight against her neck. Standing hour after endlessly dull hour on the dressmaker's platform until her legs turn to jelly. The thought is hideous but not exactly *scary*.

Next she imagines Profesora Colibrí draping a garland of apple blossoms around her shoulders and naming her the Fairest of the F.A.I.R. How the entire academy would watch her every move, ready to tally any mistake or misstep. The corner of her mouth twitches.

She imagines Mamá's carriage rattling up to the gates. Mamá catching her with a spell book and a head full of schemes. She can picture Mamá's face, a storm of anger and embarrassment.

Dominga purses her lips and blows.

At the sound of her sharp, sure whistle,

starlings and sparrows, robins and wrens swoop down from the branches and circle the oak.

"Profesora?" Jacinta shouts, scrambling back to the ground. "Something's happening!"

Profesora Colibrí, who by now has wandered to the other side of the clearing, spins around and flits back to the oaks.

"It's working!" Dominga leaps to her feet. The spell book tumbles off her lap and into the mud.

Dalia stands too, takes Dominga by the wrist, and together, they run toward the screeching swirl of birds. "¡Vamos!" she hollers, pulling her wand from her hair and raising it. *Let's go!*

But a moment later, she stops, so suddenly that Dominga stumbles forward into a clumsy somersault.

"Oh no," Dalia says, looking up.

Dominga dusts off her skirt and climbs back to

her feet. She looks to the sky where the flock of songbirds has shifted directions and is now flying straight *toward them*.

There they are! the birds shriek. They carry acorns in their beaks and claws.

"Take cover!" Dalia yells. She and Dominga tear back toward the pond. Without slowing, Dominga reaches down and picks up her spell book, using it to shield her head from the shower of acorns raining down on them.

They keep running till they get to a hollowed-out tree trunk near the blackberry bramble. They dive inside, panting.

"What went wrong?" Dominga asks. There are too many birds chattering all at once for her to understand what they're saying. It is like when Mamá gives her too many instructions in one breath and she can't tell which to follow first.

"They believed our danger calls," Dalia explains, still huffing. "But they think *we* are the danger!"

Disappointment turns to triumph as Dominga realizes what this means. "We are! Aren't we?"

Outside, one last acorn plonks down on the log, and the angry squawking of birds grows distant.

"I think it's safe to go out now," Dalia says.

"PRINCESAS!"

Not quite.

Dalia and Dominga crawl out of the log.

Profesora Colibrí stands in the grass, smacking her fan against her palm. "I admire your commitment to birdcalls, but you must be more careful," she tells them. "Think of the chaos you might have caused."

Dominga *is* thinking of it. It could have been a truly magnificent mess. She sighs.

"I can see you regret this unfortunate—" Profesora Colibrí begins.

"Look!" Jacinta and the other Sapphire princesas come running up behind Profesora Colibrí before she can finish her lecture. Their hands are full of acorns. "With all the nuts those birds dropped," Jacinta says, "we have enough to feed the chipmunks and even the hedgehogs too! Gracias, Dalia. Gracias, Dominga." She curtsies to each of them.

With her free hand, Profesora Colibrí plucks an acorn off the top of Jacinta's pile, tosses it in the air, and catches it. She beams down at Dalia and Dominga. "It seems I was mistaken," she said. "This accident was really assistance. Bravo!"

She flutters her fan and strides away. The Sapphire princesas spread out into the clearing to search for hungry creatures. Dalia and Dominga collapse against the log.

"You were right about the robins," Dominga says.

"It almost worked," Dalia says. "Until it didn't."

Dominga looks out at the spindly towers of the B.A.D., rising in the distance over a green-gray fog. "How will we ever get there?" she wonders aloud.

Dalia yips.

It is not the answer Dominga expected. She might be mistaken, but it sounds suspiciously like hyena cub for "Breakfast time!"

Yet that makes hardly any sense at all.

"I'm sorry," Dominga says, hating to admit yet another of her shortcomings, "but I don't know very much hyena. Do you mind repeating that?"

"Not hyena," Dalia replies. "Fire ant." She rubs

her ankle where the ant stung her. She searches the ground. "There you are."

Dominga half expects her to squish it. Instead, Dalia guides the insect onto her wand. She lifts it close to her nose and peers down. "But where did you come from?"

Dominga gets up and scans the dirt around them. "Aha!" Her finger pokes through a hole in her black lace glove as she points to a low mound of dirt. "Anthill."

Dalia escorts the ant, still scurrying along her wand, back to the hill.

"Safe and sound," she whispers as it wobbles back home. "With all your friends." She pauses. "*So* many friends."

She leans in and examines the hill more closely. *A bit too close*, Dominga thinks. Dalia may be in for another sting. She walks over to warn her.

"Don't you agree," Dalia says once they're standing side by side again, "that this ant seems to have an *awful* lot of friends?"

Together they watch as red ants march in and out of the hill, antennae waving. There are thousands of them. Maybe even millions.

Dominga begins to see what she suspects Dalia has already noticed. "Yes!" she says. "An *awful* lot."

A fresh plot brews. A new scheme simmers.

"What this class needs—" Dalia begins.

"Is fire ants," Dominga finishes.

CHAPTER
7

Fire ants to frighten off the hungry chipmunks. To get back at those screeching songbirds. And, most of all, to scurry up under the princesas' satin gloves and down into their silk slippers.

To bite.

To sting.

"It would be dreadful," Dalia says.

"Definitely," Dominga agrees.

Once they hear of it, the head villains of the

B.A.D. will dispatch their fastest ravens with enrollment invitations addressed to Dalia and Dominga. Perhaps they will even send a wolf-drawn carriage to deliver the ex-princesas to the tower, where they will be welcomed with one of the academy's infamous Balls for the Banished. So far, Dominga has only read about them. Still, when she closes her eyes, she can already taste the poison-flavored candied apples. She can almost hear the scrape of ghostly fingernails against the sour-noted piano keys.

Dalia clears her throat.

"Oh!" Dominga says. "Was I getting ahead of myself?"

If they want to get anywhere near the B.A.D., they must first lure a horde of angry fire ants into the forest clearing. It must happen before the end of Woodland Wildlife class.

"When the rest of the princesas have gathered to deliver their presentations would be best," Dominga says.

"It won't be easy," Dalia replies, exactly as Dominga feared she might. She waits for Dalia to explain whatever it is she has overlooked this time.

"Fire ants are even cleverer than robins," Dalia says. She points the tip of her wand at a line of ants marching single file in and out of the hill. Some carry acorn crumbs that the chipmunks left behind. "And they'll do anything to protect their queen. They won't leave the colony without a very good reason."

"Their queen?" Dominga mutters. "I bet no one sent *her* to princess school."

Dalia snickers.

It is the first time someone has laughed at one of

her jokes, and Dominga can't help but smile. She turns away and digs into her pocket for her spell book so that Dalia can't see how proud she feels.

"So," she says, recovering. "What would it take to get them out?" She opens to her page of Wicked Schemes and crosses out *Robin Ruckus*. She draws another black dot and writes *Ant Attack* next to it.

"Hmmm." Dalia taps her wand against her leg. "If they thought their home was in danger, they would storm out to defend it."

"Yes!" Dominga grins and quickly sketches a picture of the anthill. Next she draws the two of them, crouched side by side behind the blackberry bush and flicking acorns at the hill with birch-branch slingshots.

She holds the drawing out for Dalia to see.

The corners of Dalia's mouth droop. "Effective," she says, "only I hate to damage their home."

Dalia has a point. It is a rather magnificent ant-hill. She takes the book back and scribbles over her sketch. "Any other ideas?"

"They would leave for food," Dalia suggests. "If it was good enough."

Dominga scans the clearing for a suitable fire ant feast. There are the blackberries, but she noticed earlier that they are not quite ripe. Dalia still has some earthworms left over, but Dominga doubts they would be very tempting.

"Maybe we don't need food at all. Perhaps you could whisper a rumor." As soon as she says it aloud, the idea begins to swell. "Tell them there is food in the clearing! All their favorite snacks! Whatever fire ants love best."

Dalia holds a finger to her lips. "Shh," she reminds Dominga. Then she shakes her head.

Yet again.

"What's wrong this time?" Dominga asks.

"Even if I could speak perfect fire ant—and I don't—they'd never take my word for it," Dalia says. "They'll send scouts to investigate first." She steps back, unlaces her boot, and peeks inside. "I had some pastry left over, but it appears Don Ignacio has already eaten it."

Dominga looks up. "What did you say?"

"Don Ignacio," Dalia repeats. "My lizard."

"No, I mean about the pastry."

"I saved a little," Dalia says, retying her boot. "From breakfast."

Of course.

"That's it!" Dominga drops to the ground. Head bent over her spell book, she sketches out a new scheme as it takes shape in her mind. She waves Dalia over.

First, they will sneak away to the palace

pastelería. "That's the bakery," Dominga explains, in case Dalia does not already know.

Dalia nods. "Continue."

Next, they will borrow a tablecloth from the linen cupboard. They will pile pastries from the bakery on top of it—whatever they can find. Surely there must be mountains of sweets.

"Babka and bizcochitos," Dalia suggests. "That's what I used to feed the rats in Abuela and Abuelo's castle."

Dominga writes it down. She really must ask Dalia about her home sometime. *Empanadas and éclairs*, she adds underneath.

"Kolache and Kringle!" Dalia shouts.

Dominga stops writing. "You get the picture."

When the bundle is full, they will haul it back to the clearing for the princesas—and the fire ants—to find.

"Well?" Dominga asks. She holds her breath, wondering what flaw in her plan Dalia might find this time.

Dalia blows her curls off her face. "The princesas will be so delighted with their picnic that they won't notice the ants until it is too late!"

Dalia and Dominga will be admitted to the B.A.D. for certain, and maybe even placed into advanced villain classes.

"Are we agreed?" Dominga asks, holding out her hand.

"Agreed," Dalia says, shaking it.

It is settled.

"Let's go!" Dominga yells, leaping off the ground.

"Go where?" warbles Profesora Colibrí, flitting back to them.

CHAPTER 8

Dalia pinches the bridge of her nose.

Drat, Dominga thinks. Too loud. Yet again.

"Huk-huk hork," Dalia mutters under her breath. It is perfect turkey vulture for "Hush and let me handle this."

"Of course," Dominga replies. But the next thing she knows, Dalia is tiptoeing away, leaving Dominga on her own to deal with Profesora Colibrí. It is a truly villainous betrayal.

Dominga cannot decide whether this is a good thing or a bad thing.

I'm sure she'll come right back, she thinks as Profesora Colibrí approaches.

But Dominga watches in growing bewilderment as Dalia does not come back. Instead, she kneels and begins drawing squiggly lines in the dirt with her wand. To be perfectly honest, this seems rather unhelpful.

"Princesas?" Profesora Colibrí is steps away.

Dominga has no choice but to manage this herself. She lifts up her chin and makes herself as tall as she can. She slips her spell book back into her pocket, then wipes her sweaty palms on her long satin skirt. She checks to make sure her tiara is straight, which it is, of course, thanks to Inés's hairpins.

Profesora Colibrí stops in front of her. She

smiles, fan fluttering. "You two seem rather busy. Have you found a new subject for your presentation? May I see what you've finished so far?"

Dominga cannot let the profesora find the anthill. She opens her mouth, but at the worst possible moment, her words, like Dalia, abandon her. "I . . . we . . . um . . . you see . . ."

Profesora Colibrí's smile begins to flatten. She snaps her fan shut. "Princesa Dominga," she says, staring sternly down her long, thin nose. "I hope you are not leaving your presentation for the last moment. All the other princesas are hard at work. I would hate to have to deduct gems for poor time management. I would hate to have to *inform your mamá*."

Dominga gulps, remembering her mother's warning. She digs into her pockets, desperate to find something to satisfy Profesora Colibrí. An acorn cap or even a robin feather. But she knows there is nothing there but her spell book—which she dare not show—and the piece of obsidian that the profesora has already dismissed.

"Princesa Dominga, I *told* you the tracks did not lead to these rocks," Dalia says, running up behind her. "They go that way, into the pine trees."

"You told me *what?*" Dominga cannot disguise her confusion.

Dalia curtsies at Profesora Colibrí. "We have discovered some new tracks," she says, pointing toward the squiggly lines she drew in the dirt. "A rat snake, I think."

Not snake tracks, but *fake* tracks. Heading back through the forest and toward the palace. *Very sneaky.* Dominga exhales. Her jaw relaxes.

"Rat snakes are excellent climbers," Dalia

71

continues. "We should be going if we want to catch it."

Profesora Colibrí squints at the tracks. She takes a step closer.

Dominga leans toward Dalia. "I wish I had thought of that," she whispers. What if Dalia decides she is a terrible villain (and not the good kind of terrible)? What if she leaves Dominga behind, but for real this time?

"You did think of it," Dalia whispers back. "The hoofprints, remember? I simply replicated your ruse."

Dominga can't decide whether she's more surprised that Dalia noticed or that she really *had* thought of it first.

"What was that?" Profesora Colibrí demands.

"Nothing, Profesora," Dominga replies, feeling bolder now, braver. She nudges Dalia with her elbow. "We were only practicing our hisses. For when we find that snake."

Dalia tosses her hair over her face to hide her giggle.

"And Princesa Dalia is right," Dominga adds. "We better hurry." She curtsies. "Con permiso."

But Profesora Colibrí does not give her permission. She doesn't budge. Her gleaming black eyes follow the tracks to where they disappear down a dark and narrow path through the towering pine trees. She opens her fan and waves it slowly.

"It is only your second day," she says, "and the palace grounds are vast. We wouldn't want you to get lost."

"We won't get lost!" Dominga insists. "We have—" She almost tells Profesora Colibrí about Paloma's map, but thinks better of it. She is growing more cunning with every minute. "We have an excellent sense of direction. Both of us."

Dalia links her arm through Dominga's. "And we have each other," she says. "We'll stick together."

Profesora Colibrí is still not convinced. "I will summon one of the older princesas to escort you." She puts her fingers to her mouth, about to whistle.

Dalia and Dominga look at each other, panicked. They can't have an older student following them. It will ruin everything.

Dalia grabs Dominga's wrist again. Dominga senses she is about to flee. But before they can take off, someone shouts. "Profesora!"

The three of them turn toward the blackberry bush where another Opal princesa waves from her wheelchair.

"What is it, Princesa Leonor?" Profesora Colibrí calls back.

"It's these berries," Leonor says. "We need your advice. They look safe to eat, but what if they're *poisonous?*"

"Poisonous?" Profesora Colibrí freezes. "Don't eat a thing! I will be there in a moment!"

First, she gazes down at Dalia and Dominga. "I suppose a princesa should have a sense of adventure. You may go. But stay within shouting distance."

Dominga glances at Leonor, still waiting behind Profesora Colibrí. Leonor *winks*. Could she be a—

Dominga doesn't have time to finish the thought. Dalia yanks her arm. "Gracias, Profesora," she says, pulling Dominga toward the tracks. "And don't worry. We'll be *terribly* careful."

CHAPTER 9

It doesn't look much like a bakery. It certainly doesn't smell like one either. Dalia and Dominga stop outside a tiny stone cottage with a thatched roof. Its narrow windows are too high for them to see inside. Dominga looks at the map again. For someone so perfect, Paloma has very messy handwriting. No wonder she needs someone to write her letters.

"This should be the place," Dominga says. She

adjusts her glasses, which have slipped down her nose.

Unless . . . it is a trap. Would Paloma have drawn a map purposely designed to lead her sister into trouble? A plot like that would be impressive, Dominga thinks, if it weren't so impossible.

When Mamá still read them fairy tales at night, Dominga's mind used to wander—until Mamá got to the parts with the villains. Villains weren't perfect. They didn't even try to be. They didn't worry about making mistakes or fitting in. Villains could surprise you.

There was nothing surprising about a princesa like Paloma, though. Night after night, she listened to Mamá with her diary open and her pen ready to copy down any new Rules for Royalty she heard in the stories. As far as Dominga can tell, Princesa Perfecta has never broken a single one of them.

Her portrait still hangs beneath a garland of moonflowers in Casita Opal's sitting room. Paloma wouldn't risk her reputation, even now.

And yet, this does not look like any bakery Dominga has ever seen.

Dalia shrugs. "Let's find out what's inside, at least." She runs up to the cottage's heavy oak door and pushes.

It doesn't open.

She leans her shoulder into the door and pushes again. Still, it does not budge.

"I think . . ." she says, straining, "it's stuck." She falls to the ground in a heap of dirt-streaked silk.

Dominga closes the spell book and puts it back in her pocket. She studies the door, from its moss-stained bottom to its rough-edged top. Trap or not, she has listened to enough of Mamá's stories to know there might be a reason this door is shut tight. Some danger waiting on the other side. Or a secret someone wants to keep hidden.

"We shouldn't disturb it," she mumbles. As soon as the words leave her mouth, Dominga realizes they sound exactly like Paloma's rules.

"*What?*" Dalia asks, leaning up on her elbows.

"I mean . . ." Dominga begins. "I mean . . . we probably shouldn't disturb it *if* we want to be perfect princesas. But we don't, of course. We're villains. And villains go wherever they please."

She walks over to Dalia and extends an arm to help her up. "Shall we try again?"

"Together," Dalia agrees. She takes Dominga's hand and pulls herself to her feet.

Side by side, they lean into the door. This time, it creaks open.

What they find behind the door is definitely not a bakery. It doesn't seem to be a trap either.

It is a chicken coop.

They step inside and a cloud of feathers rises at their feet. Hens cluck restlessly from their roosts. One of them swoops over Dominga, smacking her tiara with a flap of her wings. Two more jump down and begin pecking at her feet. Dominga skitters backward and ducks into a corner.

She pulls the spell book out of her pocket again and opens it to Paloma's map. "Don't worry," she calls out to Dalia, running her finger over the page as she tries to figure out where they are. "I will have us back on the path in no time."

Dalia doesn't answer.

Dominga holds the pages up to the light that pours through one of the small square windows at the top of the coop. What she sees makes her breath catch and her stomach flip. All this time, she has been looking at the map *upside down*.

"I am . . . afraid . . ." she sputters, "afraid I have made a mistake. But I can fix it! I see where we need to go now."

Still, Dalia does not reply. Could she be so angry that she is refusing to speak with Dominga?

Dominga lifts her head, expecting to be met with glare of annoyance. Or a frown of disappointment. Or, even worse, a mix of both. Instead she finds Dalia clucking softly to a black-and-white-speckled hen she has scooped off the straw-strewn ground.

"This one doesn't like all the racket in here," she says. "She'd prefer to come along with us." The bird tucked under her arm, Dalia walks out of the coop without another word.

Dominga's mouth falls open. The chicken

cannot come with them. She will make noise and drop feathers—and who knows what else. In other words, she'll get them caught.

"It's a very lovely chicken, of course," she tries to explain, pulling the door shut behind them and scrambling to catch up with Dalia. "Only, I'm not sure it's very sensible for her to join our quest."

Dalia trots ahead. She picks a beetle off the ground and feeds it to the hen. "The chicken won't be any trouble," she says. "You'll hardly know she's there."

The palace clock chimes the quarter hour. Profesora Colibrí—not to mention Princesa Inés— will start looking for them soon. They must hurry. The bird will only slow them down.

"But we're running out of time, and we don't even know where we're—" Dominga begins to protest.

The hen interrupts her with an impatient squawk.

Dalia nods, then glances back at Dominga. "She says the palace bakery is just around this bend."

Dominga holds the map up to her nose. "Are you sure? Because it looks like . . ." And then she sees that the chicken is correct.

CHAPTER
10

Dalia and Dominga poke their heads into the bakery—the *actual* bakery this time. It appears to be empty, with a low fire crackling underneath the brick stove that stands along the wall across from the entrance. Baskets full of roasted nuts and fresh fruits hang from the ceiling beams, and at the center of the room is a long, sturdy table, dusty with flour. Cinnamon and sugar sweeten the air.

The hen jumps out of Dalia's arms and flaps to a shelf, just above their heads. Dalia and Dominga curtsy their thanks. The bird ruffles her feathers and settles in for a nap, camouflaged between two dull iron pots.

"Here we are," Dalia says. "Now what?"

Dominga reviews her plan. They need a tablecloth. Although she has never visited this kitchen, it looks very much like the one in her mamá's castle. She supposes all castles must be more or less the same. How dreadfully dull. Not like a villain's lair, which can be original. *Unusual*, even.

Right inside the door, she spots what must be the linen cupboard. Stepping slowly to quiet the click of her boots on the tiled floor, Dominga enters the kitchen. She opens the cupboard. Folded neatly on the bottom shelf are cloth napkins in the colors of each Casita. Deep red for the

Rubies, dark blue for the Sapphires, rich green for the Emeralds, and shimmering white for the Opals. Dominga wonders briefly if there is time to toss them all into the big copper pot that simmers on the stove. Probably not.

Placemats are stored on a shelf in the middle, and there, at the very top, are the tablecloths, too high to reach.

"I wonder if your chicken might help," Dominga suggests. Villains, she knows, often have animal minions to assist them. She has never heard of one keeping a *chicken*. But surely the B.A.D. wouldn't mind. Especially if a chicken is all they have. What's proper for a villain isn't the same as for a princesa.

"She wouldn't like to be disturbed," Dalia answers. "Not in the middle of a nap." She drops her voice to a whisper. "Besides, chickens are not great flyers and awful at fetch." She pauses. "Perhaps I could carry you on my shoulders instead?"

Dominga gauges the distance. "Still not high enough." She looks around the kitchen for supplies. "We need something to make you taller."

"A *spell*?" Dalia asks, standing up on tiptoe.

Dominga wishes she were experienced enough to cast a spell. "Not exactly."

Lined up under the table are glass jars of preserved fruits. Dominga selects the two tallest, filled with peaches, and carries them, one under each arm, to the cupboard. She knots some napkins together and uses them to attach the jars to the bottoms of Dalia's boots like stilts.

"There," she says, securing the last knot. "That should hold."

Dalia looks down uncertainly at her feet. She

lifts one of them and then the other. "If you say so."

She crouches and, once Dominga has climbed on her shoulders, staggers toward the shelf.

Dominga stretches both arms and all her fingers, reaching for the corner of the nearest tablecloth. She is so close, but still not high enough.

"Do you have it yet?" Dalia groans. "These jars are a bit slippery. And I think . . . one of the napkins . . . is coming loose."

If only Dominga had more tools. She realizes she does! "Do you think," she asks, trying to hold on as Dalia sways dangerously left and right, "I could knock one down if I threw my tiara at it?"

Dalia does not answer, except for some grunty noises that may or may not be warthog for "Might as well try" or "At least then it'd be good for *something.*" Dominga takes this as a yes. She grasps her tiara and pulls, but it does not come off. Of course—the hairpins! Somehow Inés has managed to spoil things without even being here.

"Not much longer now!" Dominga calls down to Dalia, yanking out the pins. They plink as they hit the floor far below.

At last, the tiara comes loose. Dominga closes one eye and sticks out her tongue. She pulls back her arm and takes aim.

She is about to fling the tiara when Dalia lurches forward. Dominga looks down, barely able to hold on. Dalia is slipping on the hairpins!

"Steady!" Dominga yells. "Find your balance!"

But it is no use. Dalia, with Dominga still clinging to her shoulders, topples backward—right into Chef Luís-Esteban.

"Princesas!" he barks. "What are you doing here?"

Dominga picks herself up off the floor while Dalia steps out of the stilts. Clumsily, Dominga puts her tiara back on and begins, "Well, you see . . ." This is going to be very difficult to explain.

It doesn't matter because Chef Luís-Esteban isn't listening anyway. "I called for kitchen assistants to stir the apples for tomorrow's empanadas!" he says. "Not to reorganize the linen cupboard!" He flings an apron at Dominga and another at Dalia. "Put those on. Quickly." He claps twice.

"But, Chef—" Dominga objects.

"¡Rápidamente!" He claps again, then turns on his heel and marches toward the stove.

Dalia shrugs and slips the apron over her head. Dominga helps her tie the strings.

CHAPTER 11

Back in the forest clearing, a fire ant scout, still dizzy after being dropped from a wand onto her hill, prepares to venture out again in search of food.

Nearby, Princesa Leonor sits with her water-colors behind a wooden easel. Profesora Colibrí has finally wandered off after a tiresome speech about berry safety, and Leonor can get back to her art. She glances at the blackberry bush she has been painting. She dips her brush into the green paint and adds some yellow, attempting to match the color of its leaves. As she studies, she can't help but notice the plump red berry hanging there, just waiting to be plucked.

Leonor's stomach gurgles. She should have snuck an extra pastelito or éclair into her pocket after breakfast. She looks past the canvas and toward the dark winding path that leads to the palace—the path those two strange princesas, Dalia and Dominga, just ran down. She overheard them say something about pastries. For people who seemed to be hatching a secret plot, they were awfully loud.

Leonor had hoped they would bring her back a pastelito to thank her for saving them from Profesora Colibrí with that silly story about poison berries. And even if they didn't, perhaps they'd at least liven up this class that turned terribly tedious ever since Inés assigned them all jobs. Leonor loved to paint. She did not love to be ordered around.

But Dalia and Dominga have not come back. They seem to have forgotten about her. And the pastries.

Leonor returns to her painting. With three swift swishes, she finishes the blackberry leaves, with their pointy tips and jagged edges. She swirls her brush in a glass of water to rinse it, then mixes red with blue for a color exactly like blackberry juice. Sweet blackberry juice. Her stomach growls again, this time more insistently.

Leonor peeks at the berry again. So red. So sweet. She sets the watercolors down on the tray beside her and pushes closer to the bramble. She reaches for the berry.

She almost has it when a fan snaps shut with a loud click.

Leonor freezes. She drops her arm. She turns her head, already knowing who's behind her.

"The red berry is not a ripe berry," Profesora Colibrí trills, her shining black eyes blinking fast. "Have you forgotten already, Princesa? We went over this only moments ago."

"No, Profesora."

"Remember," Profesora Colibrí says, "unless you want a bitter berry . . ."

". . . wait and pick a better berry," Leonor recites.

Profesora Colibrí nods. "Bueno. Continue with your work." She waves her fan open again and flutters it as she strolls toward the pond.

Leonor picks up her watercolors and her brush. She breathes in deeply and tries to focus on the painting. Inés warned her that it had to be perfect. She even made Leonor erase the two eerie towers of the B.A.D. she had sketched into the background. Leonor had thought they made the painting more exciting. Inés insisted they absolutely did not belong.

"Exactly what do you think you're doing?"

Leonor shudders. It is almost as if she has begun to hear Inés's voice in her head. She lifts her hand and adds a small violet dot to her canvas.

"I *said*, '*What* do you think you're doing?'"

Leonor startles, leaving a red-blue streak across her painting. She *does* hear Inés. And not just in her head. She's snuck up beside her.

Leonor sighs. "I am painting the blackberries," she says, without looking at Inés. She takes a sponge from her tray of art supplies and dabs at the streak of paint. "Just like you told me to do."

Inés steps between Leonor and the canvas. "I *mean*, what do you think you're doing eating those blackberries? Do you want Profesora Colibrí to think Casita Opal has not been paying attention? Do you want her to take gems from our golden chalice? Do you want us to *LOSE*?"

With each question, Inés leans in closer, and her nose turns pinker. It would make a very nice shade for a berry, Leonor thinks. She adds a little more red paint to the mixture on her palette. When she is satisfied it matches Inés's nose exactly, she reaches around her and continues painting. "Of course not," she answers. "All I want is to create a *marvelous* masterpiece. Exactly like you wanted. If you'll excuse me."

Maybe if she appears busy enough, Inés will go away and Leonor will get another chance at that berry.

But Inés does not go away.

She paces in front of Leonor, blocking her view of the bramble.

"Is there something else?" Leonor asks after a while. "It's difficult to paint with you standing there."

Inés folds her arms. "Have you seen Princesa Dominga lately? Her sister was last year's Fairest of the F.A.I.R., you know. She probably has all sorts of secrets for getting ahead here, but she isn't sharing them, which isn't proper princess behavior, if you ask me. In fact, I am beginning to wonder if there's something a little bit diff—" Inés stops in the middle of her ramble. She touches her tiara, which sits perfectly balanced atop her red hair. "Anyway, do you know where she went?"

Leonor waits before answering. Her father has told her it is wise to pause and collect one's thoughts. Especially in a complicated situation like this one. She does not want to give Dalia and Dominga away, especially while there are still pastelitos on the line. On the other hand, she *does* very much want to be rid of Inés.

"Well," she says, after she's decided the best course of action. "Now that you mention it, I saw her not too long ago. She was with that princesa from Casita Emerald—the one who talks to bullfrogs. They were heading that way." She nods toward the path and the dark stand of pine trees.

Inés scowls.

"Profesora Colibrí told them to stay within shouting distance," Leonor continues. "But . . ." She cups her hands around her mouth and shouts in the direction of the path. "Hello?"

Leonor and Inés listen for a reply. None comes. Inés's scowl deepens.

"They'll get caught!" she growls, stomping her satin slipper. "They'll cost us gems!"

Leonor adds more strokes to her painting. "Probably," she says. "Unless . . ."

Inés leans in closer again. So close Leonor can count the freckles on her nose and cheeks. So close she could paint in even more freckles if she wanted. She forces herself to lower her brush.

"Unless?"

"Unless they are lost," Leonor explains. "Think of the gems you would earn for bringing them back safely."

Inés straightens. She stares into the forest, picking at the edges of her pink silk gloves.

Leonor starts painting again.

"It's awfully dark," Inés says. "We'll go together. You and I."

Leonor was afraid this might happen. She

rinses her brush and begins packing up her paints as she decides what to say next.

"I would *love* to go with you," she says. "I could use the extra gems Profesora Colibrí would give me for helping. I'm sure you don't need *all* of them."

Inés presses her lips together. "On second thought, *I'll* go," she says. "You'll stay here to keep working. You have an awful lot to do before that painting is perfect."

Leonor fights to hide her smile. "You're quite right," she says. "As usual."

While Inés marches away, Leonor tilts her head and considers her canvas. What had started as a painting of a blackberry bramble has turned into a slice of blackberry pie. With a scoop of vanilla ice cream on top.

Her stomach grumbles again.

How bitter could a berry be? she asks herself.

She glances over her shoulder to make sure Profesora Colibrí isn't watching. She checks behind her to be sure Inés is too far away to see. She reaches into the bramble. She plucks the berry. She pops it into her mouth.

Her eyes squinch shut. Her lips pucker. The answer to her question is *very, very bitter.* But not *bad* exactly. She swallows and reaches for another.

CHAPTER
12

Dalia and Dominga stand at the stove. Still stuck inside the palace bakery, they take turns stirring the pot of apple slices, the way Chef Luís-Esteban showed them.

The pastries left over from breakfast are tantalizingly near. They sit piled on racks beside the stove, waiting to be chopped into pieces for tonight's bread pudding.

Dalia and Dominga must get to them—and get

out of here—before that happens. But whenever they try, Chef Luís-Esteban looks up from rolling dough and snarls.

At the moment the chef is humming quietly to himself, the melody interrupted by occasional grumbles. Dalia nudges Dominga. Dominga nods in reply. It is time to make another attempt. She passes the spoon to Dalia.

Dominga tiptoes backward toward the pastries, keeping one eye on Chef Luís-Esteban. For once she would have preferred a pair of satin slippers like Inés's. They would land more lightly on the clay tiles.

She takes one wary step. And then another. Dalia stirs the apples more wildly, letting the spoon clang against the side of the pot to cover the sound of Dominga's boots.

After another step, Dominga is close enough

to smell the sticky-sweet guava in the pastelitos. She reaches.

She almost has the pastry when the heel of her boot crunches down on a walnut shell.

"Princesa!" Chef Luís-Esteban barks. "Why have you left the stove? You must watch the filling carefully. If it burns, it will be ruined!" Dalia and Dominga exchange a glance. Burning the filling is not an entirely bad idea. (Or rather, it is very bad, but that is what makes it so *good*.)

But it will have to wait. For now. Dominga wipes her palms on her skirt. "Well ... I ..." Her eyes dart around the kitchen, searching for an excuse. They land on the spice rack. "Cinnamon," she says, facing Chef Luís-Esteban again. "The apples need more cinnamon."

The chef frowns, sets down his rolling pin, and stomps toward them, a flurry of flour floating around his head. Dominga shuffles backward, but Dalia's feet stay planted on the tile. When Chef Luís-Esteban holds out his hand for the spoon, she sets it on his palm.

He fishes out a chunk of apple, picks it off the spoon, and drops it in his mouth. As he chews, he closes his eyes and hums some more.

His eyes pop open. "You're right!" he shouts.

"I am?" Dominga asks.

Although Chef Luís-Esteban's voice is gruff, it is still more pleasant than Mamá's when she used to watch Dominga cook, always warning her not to use the good silver, or complaining that she'd scorched another saucepan. And then there was that time one of Dominga's potion experiments exploded over the stove and Mamá had banished her from the kitchen for good.

"More cinnamon!" Chef Luís-Esteban orders.

Dominga hurries to retrieve the cinnamon from the spice rack. She twists open the jar and pulls out a stick.

Chef Luís-Esteban grunts in approval and lumbers back to his dough. Before he begins rolling again, he looks at Dalia. "And you," he says. "Stir more gently. We are not *angry* at the apples. The apples have done nothing wrong."

Dominga picks up the spoon Chef Luís-Esteban left behind and takes her turn at the pot. Slowly, the mixture begins to thicken into a golden-brown and bubbly goo. Dominga cannot help but dream of the potions she'll stir someday at the B.A.D.

If she ever makes it there. If she ever makes it out of this kitchen.

After a few more minutes, Chef Luís-Esteban lifts his nose and sniffs the air. He walks back to the stove, takes the spoon from Dominga, and scoops up more of the filling.

This time, when he closes his eyes to taste the apples, Dalia's hand shoots up to the shelf above the stove, so fast it is only a blur. When Chef Luís-Esteban opens his eyes again, Dalia's hand is in her pocket. She winks at Dominga.

Chef Luís-Esteban smacks the spoon against the bricks. "Perfecto!" he cries. "Ten gems for Casita Opal!"

"*Perfecto?*" Dominga repeats. *Ten gems?* She remembers Profesora Colibrí's speech from the previous morning. The Casita with the most gems at the end of the term will earn a pass to venture off the palace grounds. Even if all their schemes fail—as this one seems doomed to—Dominga might *still* be able to escape to the B.A.D. tower.

Not with Dalia, though. Dalia is in Casita

Emerald, and if the Opals win, she wouldn't be able to come. Dominga shakes the idea from her mind. She can't leave Dalia behind, not after all they've been through.

"Pour the manzanas into a bowl," Chef Luís-Esteban says. "I will go light the ovens."

As soon as his back is turned, Dalia dips her finger into the pot for a taste.

"The apples are terribly sweet," she says with a scowl.

Dominga makes sure Chef Luís-Esteban isn't watching and sneaks a taste too. Dalia is right. The apples are very sweet—but also quite tasty.

Dalia pushes her hair off her face and arches an eyebrow. "Perhaps we can improve them." She reaches into her pocket and pulls out a jar of pickled jalapeños. The one she snatched from the shelf when Chef's eyes were closed.

"That would ruin the filling!" Dominga gasps.

"I know," Dalia says, already twisting open the jar. "Something else to impress the B.A.D.! Just think how the princesas' eyes will water when they bite into these tomorrow morning."

It is a frightfully clever plot. Dominga knows this. The trouble is, no one has ever called *her* perfect before. Of course, it was actually the apple filling and not *her* that Chef Luís-Esteban had said was perfect. But still.

"What if—"

It is too late. Dalia has emptied the entire jar into the pot. The jalapeños bob at the surface a moment, then sink.

Ahem, someone coughs.

"Is it the jalapeños?" Dalia asks. "They *were* rather strong, weren't they? I'm sniffling myself."

"It wasn't me," Dominga answers.

They both turn to the door.

Two older princesas, their braids tucked neatly under hairnets, stand there.

Just then, Chef Luís-Esteban returns to the stove without noticing them. "Why haven't you poured the filling into a bowl yet?" He claps twice. "¡Rapídamente!" When Dalia and Dominga don't reply, he follows their stares to the doorway.

"Who are you?" he demands of the older princesas. "What are you doing in my kitchen?"

The princesas look at each other and roll their eyes. They step inside.

"I am Princesa Fernanda," the shorter one says with a curtsy. "And this is Princesa Beatriz. We're the kitchen assistants. You called for us?"

"We would have been here sooner," Beatriz adds, "but we got caught behind a pack of the new princesas. They were looking for a fawn."

Chef Luís-Esteban loosens the kerchief that's tied around his neck. "If you are the kitchen assistants, then who are . . ."

"I'll tell you who they are!" calls a voice from just outside the kitchen. "Villains!"

CHAPTER 13

Dominga is so stunned to see Inés standing here, so far from the forest clearing, that it takes her several moments to realize Inés is covered in feathers. White and gray, they stick out of her ringlets and cling to her yellow gown.

And when Dominga finally notices Inés is covered in feathers, she forgets that she ought to be worried about getting caught.

"You realize there are feathers in your hair?" Dominga can't help asking.

Inés's nose turns pink and she swats a clump of fluff off her tiara. "What did you expect to happen when you led me into that chicken coop?" She rushes forward. "You did it on purpose, didn't you?" She points, and when she raises her arm, another feather flutters off her glove.

Beatriz sneezes.

"Salud," Inés turns and says. Then she pivots back to Dominga. *"Didn't you?"*

Dalia looks down at Inés's silk slippers. They had started out that morning as creamy white as the filling inside Chef Luís-Esteban's éclairs. But now they are covered in grass stains and caked with mud.

Dalia snorts. "Boots would have been much more practical," she says.

Inés tries to cover her shoes under the folds of her rumpled skirt. But that only shows off the tear along one of its seams.

"Well, I hardly had time to change my shoes, did I?" Inés screeches. "Not if I was going to *rescue* you! From being *lost*! In the *FOREST*!" She stomps her feet. Beatriz and Fernanda inch toward the door as another cloud of feathers falls.

"But we're not lost," Dominga says. "We're right here."

Inés lifts her chin and grins as if she's won a game of Capture the Crown. "Precisely," she says. "You're here when you should be in the clearing helping me . . . I mean, *us* . . . win the challenge." The corners of her mouth turn down as she notices the flour in Dalia's hair and the smudge of apple filling that clouds Dominga's glasses. "It's almost as if you're not actually princesas at all."

Dominga gulps. Her hands begin to tremble. She did not mean to be discovered so soon. Dalia pinches her elbow. Dominga does not speak crab, but she imagines the pinch means something like "Keep quiet. Keep calm."

"But that doesn't matter," Inés continues. "Because now that I've caught you, I'm certain Profesora Colibrí will award me even *more* gems. A true princesa follows the rules."

Fernanda coughs politely again. She and Beatriz have taken off their aprons and folded them over their arms. "It looks like you have plenty of help in the kitchen, Chef," she says, stepping toward the door. "So we'll be on our way."

"Not so fast!" Chef Luís-Esteban roars. "I will have no travesuras in my kitchen!"

"Trah-veh-SOO-rahs?" Inés wrinkles her nose as she repeats the word slowly.

"Mischief," Dalia whispers helpfully.

"Or tricks," Dominga adds. They should know, after all.

"Princesas!" Chef Luís-Esteban roars again. "Explain yourselves!"

This time he is looking directly at Dalia and Dominga. But how can they explain themselves? It seems to Dominga that Chef Luís-Esteban, with his growling voice and snappish temper, might not exactly . . . *belong* at the F.A.I.R. either. But she doubts that even he would understand if they told the truth: that she and Dalia came to the kitchen planning a travesura so tremendous it would capture the attention of the B.A.D.

Inés doesn't give them a chance to make any excuses. "They told Profesora Colibrí they were tracking a snake," she answers for them. "But as you can see, it was all a trick. I don't know what they're up to, Chef, but I'm sure it is *dreadful*."

"Oooh," Beatriz and Fernanda say, leaning in. Fernanda scoops up a handful of toasted hazelnuts from one of the hanging baskets and pops them into her mouth, crunching as she watches to see what will happen next.

Dominga tries to ignore them. She tries to ignore her own racing heartbeat and the drops of sweat dripping down from underneath her tiara. She can already hear a lock click shut at Mamá's palace if she gets caught. She can already feel her hands cramp after days spent writing Paloma's endless letters. She can already see the towers of the B.A.D. drifting farther and farther into the distance.

"Is this true?" Chef Luís-Esteban asks.

"It's true there were tracks," Dalia answers, eyes locked on Inés. "And it's true we were following them."

Inés puts her hands on her hips. "Then where is the snake?" She raises her eyes to the ceiling and drops them down to the floor. She makes a show of craning her neck to peer around Chef Luís-Esteban into the back of the kitchen. "I don't see any snake around here."

Chef Luís-Esteban turns to Dominga. "Did you see this snake?"

He looks disappointed. Like she is not who he expected her to be. It is a look that Dominga knows well, and one she has never liked, to be honest.

Dalia brushes a wisp of black hair out of her eyes and smiles at her. *It must be easy to smile when you're already so good at being bad*, Dominga

118

thinks. *When you don't have Princesa Perfecta for an older sister.*

Dalia will get more chances to prove herself to the B.A.D. She'll probably do even better on her own. But if Dominga is caught now, before she's managed to pull off even one wicked scheme, she'll be sent home for good.

And anyway, she asks herself again, *who ever heard of a villain having a friend?*

She lets her chin fall to her chest. She looks down at the floor and focuses hard on the bits of walnut shell she crushed earlier. "No, Chef," she mumbles. "I only went because Princesa Dalia said there was one."

Dalia makes a choked sort of yelp, like Paloma's kittens when they feel cold or lonely or in need of attention. Dominga cannot bear to glance up, but even without looking, she can picture Dalia's eyes, wide with surprise and hurt.

"I knew it!" Inés says. "I knew you were one of us." She wraps her arm around Dominga's shoulder. Dominga pulls away. "Just like your sister. The Fairest of the F.A.I.R."

Chef Luís-Esteban groans, unties his neckerchief completely, and dabs his forehead with it. Then he waves the piece of cloth at Beatriz and Fernanda. "Princesas," he says, "we have wasted enough time. We must have flan! Eggs! Sugar!" He claps twice.

"And you two." He points to Inés and Dalia. "I'll have no travesuras in my kitchen. Go back to Profesora Colibrí. Tell her I require Dominga's help with the empanadas. ¡Rápidamente!"

CHAPTER 14

Fernanda scoops sugar into a measuring cup, and Beatriz cracks eggs into a bowl. Chef Luís-Esteban goes back to the dough he rolled out on the table and begins cutting it into circles while he hums.

Dominga stands still. She watches Inés and Dalia walk out the door, then listens to their footsteps in the hallway until the sound fades. She reaches into her pocket and squeezes the shiny-smooth chunk of obsidian she still carries.

It reminds her of how she had hoped to find a place to belong here. She pats the other pocket and feels her spell book. Even with Paloma's map inside, she seems to have already lost her way.

"Princesa?" Chef Luís-Esteban says, less gruffly than before.

Dominga nods and gets back to work. She pours the apple filling into a bowl and carries it to the table. Then, standing alongside Chef Luís-Esteban, she spoons a glob of apple filling into the middle of each circle of dough.

She has only done what any other villain would have, she tells herself, scooping up more apples. It's probably what Dalia would have done if she had thought of it first.

But she hadn't.

"Princesa!" Chef Luís-Esteban growls. "The filling!"

"Huh?" Dominga looks down and sees that she

has accidentally dribbled apples down the front of her apron and all over the table.

"Sorry, Chef," she apologizes with a curtsy. "I must have been distracted."

Chef Luís-Esteban grumbles and hands her the towel he carries looped through his belt.

I only have to pretend *to be a perfect princesa until the end of the term*, she tells herself, wiping up the apples. *Only long enough to help Casita Opal earn the most gems.*

Then, with the freedom to wander into the village, she'll make her escape.

She gives the bowl of filling a stir and imagines herself whipping up potions inside the dim and cobwebby kitchens of the B.A.D. When she closes her eyes, she can almost smell the putrid fumes. She can almost hear Dalia training a flock of ravens in the courtyard outside.

She stops stirring and opens her eyes. She has gotten ahead of herself. What if Dalia doesn't make it to the B.A.D. after all? Worse, what if she *does* make it, and she never wants to speak to Dominga again?

Dominga wonders if that would be even more dreadful than being locked up in Mama's palace with a quill and a pot of Perfecta's signature violet ink.

She realizes with a thick and sour taste at the back of her throat that it would.

Inés and Dalia can't have gotten very far yet. Dominga still has a chance to catch them, to save their scheme. But first she has to get out of this kitchen.

Chef Luís-Esteban pinches the empanadas closed into little half-moon shapes and arranges them on a cooking tray. Fernanda has poured the sugar into a pan and stirs it over a low flame to make caramel. Beatriz cracks another egg into the bowl.

Eggs!

Dominga wishes she had thought of it sooner. Even more than that, she wishes Dalia were still here. Dalia could pull this off as easily as the simplest sleeping potion. Not Dominga. She hasn't had enough practice. She is so far behind. But she has no choice. She must try.

She sets down her spoon. She grips the edge of the wooden tabletop to steady herself.

She clucks.

She hopes it is acceptable chicken-speak for "Pardon me, but if you're still there, I could really use some help!"

Dominga closes her mouth and listens for a response. Fernanda and Beatriz gape at her.

"What was that?" Beatriz asks, scratching her temple.

Chef Luís-Esteban tightens his jaw but continues folding the empanadas.

Dominga catches a glimpse of herself reflected in one of the big copper pots that hang from the ceiling. Her cheeks are raspberry pink and her tiara has slipped down her forehead. She has to try again. She thinks back to the way Dalia sounded inside the chicken coop, takes a breath, and clucks. Louder this time.

She hopes it comes out more or less like "Hello? Please wake up! I need a favor!"

For an unbearably long time, all Dominga can hear is the low crackle of fire under the stove and the scrape of Fernanda's wooden spatula against the saucepan.

But then, with a flap and a squawk, the

black-and-white-speckled hen swoops off the shelf near the linen closet, knocking over a sack of flour on her way down. Beatriz squeals and grabs an empty pie plate to cover her head as a blizzard of flour pours to the floor.

"This had better be important!" the chicken clucks. "You woke me up from a very nice nap!"

Before she answers, Dominga glances around the kitchen to see whether anyone else understands the bird. Beatriz and Fernanda's slowly blinking eyes and Chef Luís-Esteban's open-mouthed stare tell her they do not.

The hen struts toward Dominga. "Well? Explain yourself!"

Dominga drops her voice. She starts out slowly in her still-shaky hen-speak. "I'm very sorry to disturb you," she says. "But I wonder if you would be willing to make a scene? Cause a commotion?

Raise a ruckus? Something to distract them so I can get out of here?"

"Distract them?" the hen answers. She jumps, flaps, and lands on the counter so that she and Dominga are nearly eye to eye. "You mean like this?"

Chef Luís-Esteban howls. "Princesa! Are you speaking to this gallina? Tell her to leave! ¡Inmediatamente!" He waves his arms to shoo the bird away, but she only ducks and nibbles a bit of apple.

Dominga laughs. "Yes, please!"

"And why should I do you a favor?" the hen asks. "You were going to abandon me in the chicken coop."

"It's not only a favor for me," Dominga pleads. "It's also for Dalia . . . my *friend*." Dominga looks up just in time to see Beatriz sneaking behind the hen with the empty flour sack. "Watch out!"

The hen hops out of the way and flaps clumsily upward. "Dalia?" she asks. "Why didn't you say so?" Then she steers toward Chef Luís-Esteban. She lands on his hat, pushing it down over his eyes.

"Aaargh!" the chef yells, staggering in circles.

"I'll get her!" Fernanda shouts. She charges toward the chef with a bowl full of water from the washbasin. She takes aim and hurls the water at his head.

Before even a drop can touch her, the hen leaps away, crashing into the basket of hazelnuts. They roll across the floor like marbles. Fernanda and Beatriz wheel their arms, trying not to trip on them. But Chef Luís-Esteban, having finally pulled his hat from over his eyes, loses his balance and stumbles backward.

While Fernanda and Beatriz try to help him to his feet, Dominga dashes to the pastries. She holds her apron out in front of her and rakes them in, as quickly as she can.

"Don't worry!" she calls over her shoulder as she drops a handful of hazelnuts into her pocket. "I'll get that chicken out of here!"

When her apron is full, she hugs the bundle close to her chest. She whistles to the hen. "Let's go! It's time to fly!"

"So soon?" the hen asks. She flutters to Dominga's shoulder, and together they bolt out of the kitchen.

CHAPTER 15

"All you have to do is limp a bit," Inés tells Dalia, "and Profesora Colibrí will believe I came to your rescue." She plucks one last feather from her sleeve. "Let's face it. You certainly *look* as if you fell into a snake pit, and this way, you won't get into quite so much trouble as you would for wandering away with no excuse. You can thank me later."

Dominga has caught up to Inés and Dalia on the

pine-lined path between the palace and the forest clearing. She darts from tree to tree, watching—and listening—from several steps behind while the chicken snoozes on her shoulder. Every now and then, Dalia looks back as if she senses Dominga following her. But if she does, she isn't saying so.

Instead, Dalia snorts and marches ahead of Inés. "You're not trying to keep me out of trouble. You want me to go along with your ridiculous story because you think Profesora Colibrí will give you more gems for saving me from a snake pit than for catching me in the kitchen."

Inés skips to catch up. "And what's so wrong with that? Either way, I brought you back, didn't I?"

Dominga hurries to the next tree, careful not

to let any of the pastries fall from her apron. The chicken stirs.

"I thought princesas always told the truth," Dalia says, kicking a pine cone out of her way.

Inés pauses. She tilts her head upward, and the sun, warm and golden, glints off her tiara. "Princesas make the most of every situation," she says, then starts walking again. "In fact, it would be *wrong* to ignore this chance to help my Casita. To help *you*." Just ahead of her, Dalia stomps in a puddle. Mud splatters the bottom of Inés's gown.

Dominga claps a hand over her mouth to hide her cackle. She nearly drops the pastries.

Inés grinds her teeth together and growls.

"And because I am so *generous*," she goes on, "I'll tell Profesora Colibrí that you were trying to protect the snakes from a badger." She smiles, pleased with herself. "Yes, a badger. Maybe she'll award you some gems too. Not as many as she'll give me, of course. But some."

Dalia whirls to face Inés. Her dark green skirt billows out around her. "I don't want any gems, and I don't need your help. I'll figure this out. *On my own!*"

She says the last part louder than the rest, and Dominga winces. She wonders again whether Dalia suspects she is there. Whether Dalia would rather she were someplace else.

Dominga starts to turn back. The pastries are getting heavy anyway, especially with a chicken asleep on her shoulder.

Then she looks down at the bundle of pastelitos and pan dulce. It really was a deliciously dreadful plot, she thinks. A true villain would keep trying. And even if Dalia doesn't want to be a team anymore, at least Dominga can free her from Inés's clutches.

She wiggles her shoulder to rouse the hen. "It's time," she clucks softly.

The bird blinks and raises her head. "Already?" she squawks. "I was in the middle of a rather enjoyable dream."

"I'm sorry," Dominga apologizes. "But if we wait any longer, it will be too late."

"Very well," the chicken answers. "You've woken me up anyway."

"Thank you," Dominga says. "On the count of three. Uno . . ." The hen ruffles her feathers.

"Dos." Dominga tightens her grip around the apron.

"Tres!" Dominga springs out from behind the tree. The hen leaps from her shoulder, flaps, then dives straight for Inés's tiara.

Inés turns and shrieks. "Not more chickens!" She waves her arms. With a flick of her wing, the hen changes directions and comes to a soft landing at Dalia's feet.

Dalia crouches and scratches the chicken's head.

Inés glares at Dominga. "What are *you* doing here?"

Dalia straightens and blows the hair out of her eyes. Then she glares too. "What *are* you doing here?"

"Skreek!" Dominga screeches under her breath in feverish turkey vulture for "Now's your chance! Go!"

But Dalia doesn't move.

"And what's all that?" Inés asks, pointing at Dominga's apron, bulging with pastries.

"Never mind," Dominga says. "You're lucky I caught you in time."

"Caught *me*?" Inés asks, tossing her hair over her shoulder. "What in the palace are you talking about?"

Dominga flashes what she hopes is a blindingly brilliant princesa smile. Inés cringes and takes a step backward.

"You aren't planning to go back to class looking like *that*, are you?" Dominga replies. "A princesa should always present her most splendid self. At least that's what my sister, Paloma, says. She wrote it right here"—Dominga pats her pocket where the spell book is—"and she was the Fairest of the F.A.I.R., you know."

Inés looks down at her gown. The feathers are gone, but so are some of the glass beads that used to shimmer at the waist. The chickens must have pecked them off. Her gloves are wrinkled, and the ribbons that lace her slippers are in shreds.

"And I'm sorry to say, but you smell like a chicken coop," Dominga adds.

Inés lifts her arm and sniffs.

She frowns.

"But Profesora Colibrí will understand when she hears how I had to rescue Dalia," she says. "When she finds out how far you two wandered away from the clearing."

Dominga shrugs. "Maybe. Or maybe she'll take away even *more* gems. *Most splendid.* Paloma was very clear about that part."

Inés hesitates. Doubt dulls her normally gleaming eyes.

Dominga stretches her face into a smile so wide her cheeks hurt. "If you hurry back to the Casita now, you can clean up and return to the clearing before class ends. And if Profesora Colibrí asks where you are, I'll tell her you finally found that fawn."

Inés's eyes flash. "Tell her there was a thorn stuck in its hoof!" She gathers up her skirt. "Tell her I was the only one who knew how to help!" She races toward the Casitas, knocking into Dominga on her way past.

Once she has disappeared into the woods, Dominga sinks to the ground in relief. "It worked!" A pastelito falls out of her apron. "Oops," she says.

Dalia turns away from Dominga. "That was a rather spectacular scheme," she admits. "But it wouldn't have been necessary if you hadn't betrayed me back in the kitchen."

Dominga blows some dirt off the pastelito and drops it on top of her bundle. "I know," she says, and stands. "I'm sorry. It's just that you're already such a *perfect* villain, and I've never been very good at anything. I'm definitely not good enough for the B.A.D." Or was it *bad* enough for the B.A.D.? Either way, meeting Dalia showed Dominga how much she still has to learn. "I thought you'd leave me behind."

Dalia twists one of her long curls. "Until you left *me* behind, I thought that together, we could be even *better* at being bad," she says.

"Maybe we still can," Dominga suggests hopefully. "We have all these pastries, after all."

Dalia straightens her tiara. "And that anthill is just sitting there."

Dominga's mood lightens. Or is it darkens? She is not sure which, and it doesn't much matter. What does matter is that the plot, once again, is thickening.

CHAPTER 16

The palace clock chimes another quarter hour.

"Class will be over any moment now!" Dominga shouts. "Let's go!" She tears down the path. The toe of her boot nearly catches in a ground squirrel's hole, but she doesn't slow down. Pastelitos and pan dulce tumble from her apron. Dalia runs behind, picking up the spilled pastries and stuffing them in her pockets.

The black-and-white hen stretches her neck

and struts off the path. "I expect there'll be another racket," she clucks crankily, nestling into a crevice between two pine roots. "I'll have a better chance at a nap out here than with you two."

But Dominga can hardly hear her and Dalia, who can, isn't paying attention. She clutches her tiara to keep it from slipping off her head and gallops even faster.

Together, they jog to the edge of the clearing and stop to catch their breath. Now that it's nearly lunchtime, the sun has shrunk the shadows into small splashes of gray, none big enough for Dalia and Dominga to hide in. Instead, they crouch among the birch trees and watch.

Dalia shields her eyes with her hand and squints toward the anthill. It is still alive with ants crawling in and out of its narrow opening. At the base of the hill, a line of scouts sets out, antennae waggling as they zip in one direction and then another in search of food. "Look," Dalia says. "They're *hungry*."

Dominga crawls from the birch trees to the back side of the blackberry bush to get a better look at the princesas. She pulls apart the leaves and peers through the bramble. Princesa Leonor is still there on the other side. Her painting complete, she is rinsing out her brushes. Princesa Lizeth sits beside her on a rock. She peels off one of her mint-green gloves and dabs the back of her neck with it.

Dominga peeks over the blackberries, just long enough to see a group of princesas at the pond, adding twigs to their model of a beaver dam. In the tall grass nearby, another clump of princesas kneel beside a hedgehog, tucking bits off moss and handfuls of maple leaves into her nest.

Profesora Colibrí sits on a tree stump, fanning herself. "Make your finishing touches, princesas," she sings out, a little less chirpily than earlier. "We shall begin the presentations shortly."

Dominga ducks her head behind the bramble again. They have arrived just in time. With her free hand, Dominga fishes the bit of obsidian out of her pocket. She holds it up so it catches the light. That is her sign to Dalia. "Now!"

Dalia creeps out from behind the birch trees with a pastelito, only slightly smooshed, in her hand. She pulls off a bit of the flaky pastry and flicks it into the path of the fire ant scouts. The nearest scout stops when the crumb lands, then crawls over to investigate. It circles the pastry, tiny jaws opening and closing. Then it rushes to a nearby ant. They touch antennae before darting away to alert two more scouts. Dominga does not

know a word of their language, but she understands what this means: "We have discovered
food!"

The plot is working!

Dalia drops a trail of pastry and guava filling that leads all the way back to the shady spot
among the birch trees. The perfect place for a
picnic. Dominga joins her and opens the apron,
letting the pastelitos and pan dulce, empanadas
and éclairs fall to the ground—all but one that
she keeps in her pocket. Together, she and Dalia
arrange the pastries in neat piles.

By the time they are finished, the scouts have
returned with reinforcements. Ants pour out of
the hill like the first trickle of lava out of a volcano.
Long rust-colored lines of them march toward
the birch trees, following Dalia's trail of sweets.
There are enough to carry a whole pastelito back

to the anthill. More than enough to wreck a picnic. All that's missing are the princesas.

"I think it's time to invite the rest of our guests," Dominga says, rubbing her palms together.

Dalia nods. "I quite agree." Leaving the pastries behind, they crawl back to the blackberry bush. They listen.

"Do you suppose the palace bells might be broken?" Princesa Leonor asks. "Shouldn't we have been dismissed for lunch by now?"

Princesa Lizeth's stomach growls. "Are you *sure* none of those berries are ripe?"

The princesas are hungry too.

"Shall I?" Dalia asks, her voice so low even Dominga has to strain to hear her. She nearly nods in agreement. After all, Dalia is far better prepared for the next step in their scheme than she is.

But she pauses. She must prove—to Dalia, to the

B.A.D., and most of all to herself—that she is villain enough.

"Allow me," she says. Dominga clears her throat. She thumps the ground twice with her glove-covered knuckles, then squeaks.

An instant later, there is a rustling in the leaves, and then the scraping of tiny feet scuttling down a tree trunk.

A squirrel jumps onto Dominga's lap, twitches its nose, fluffs its gray tail, then chatters. Dominga is pretty sure it's squirrel-speak for "You say you want to make a deal?"

"Could I interest you in some hazelnuts?" Dominga chitters back. She opens her palm to reveal a handful of nuts from the basket in the kitchen. The squirrel reaches out its paw, but Dominga yanks them back. "I need you to help us first."

The squirrel flicks its tail. With her other hand, Dominga takes the last pastelito from her pocket. She pronounces the next words slowly and carefully to be sure the squirrel knows what to do. "Drag this pastry into the clearing—make sure the princesas see you—then bring it back to the birch trees."

The squirrel barks and jumps off Dominga's lap.

"No way am I going anywhere near those princesas," it chirrups. "The one in the yellow dress tried to bandage my tail!"

Dominga closes her fist and rattles the hazelnuts in her hand. "Are you sure? They're roasted," she says. "And I can get you even more."

The squirrel slinks toward her again. *"More?"*

"Loads more," Dalia promises.

The squirrel hesitates, then clicks its front

claws together and snatches the pastelito out of Dominga's hand. "Deal!"

Dalia and Dominga watch it dart through the blackberry bramble with the pastelito in its mouth. It races up a leg of Leonor's easel and perches atop it. A glob of guava drips on her canvas.

Leonor's eyes widen. "Princesa Lizeth?" she says. "Do you see a squirrel with a guava pastelito sitting on top of my easel? Or am I just *very* hungry?"

Lizeth stands. She rubs her dark brown eyes. "It's real," she replies. "And I think the pastelito is guava *and* cream cheese."

Leonor pushes closer to the easel. She reaches for the pastelito, but the squirrel chirps and scampers back down, around the bramble and toward the stand of birch trees.

"Wait!" Leonor calls out, already chasing it.

"We only want to share," Lizeth adds. *"Please?"*

"Hurry!" Dalia says. "They'll see us!" She and Dominga dive into the hollowed-out tree trunk to listen and to wait.

CHAPTER 17

Her back leaning against the inside of the hollow trunk, Dominga imagines princesas in their silks and chiffons, their ruffles and feathers, sitting down to picnic alongside a swarm of fire ants. She can almost smell the sticky salves the nurse will have to apply to their bites. She can nearly feel the invitation to join the B.A.D. finally in her hands. Her fingers tingle in anticipation.

The squirrel pokes its head through a hole in the trunk and startles her back to the present.

"My hazelnuts?" he chirps. Dominga fishes for them in her pocket, trying not to elbow Dalia in the tight space.

"Here you go," she says. "And you'll find even more inside the palace pastelería."

The squirrel stashes the hazelnuts in his cheeks and scampers away.

Dalia peers through the hole. "I don't see anything yet," she says. She slouches back down inside the trunk. "I hope I didn't bring the fire ants over too soon. The princesas won't stop at our picnic if they notice them there."

Dominga does not know what to say at first. She never imagined that Dalia, already a true villain, could doubt herself. She tries to reassure her. "They won't notice a thing," she says. "The ants are so small and the princesas are so hungry. The pastries are all they'll see." She takes off her glasses and wipes the lenses on the edge of her gown. She has her own worries about what might go wrong, but she hesitates to confess them.

"What if there aren't enough princesas?" she asks in a whisper. Two princesas, Leonor and Lizeth, stung by fire ants might be an unfortunate accident. But it is hardly a dreadful disaster. "I should have been more specific when I gave the squirrel instructions," she says. "I should have asked him to gather *all* the princesses."

"Listen," Dalia says.

"I know," Dominga replies. "I should have *listened* to my instincts and let you handle the animal sounds. I just thought that if—"

"No! Shh!" Dalia hushes her. *"Listen."* She points outside.

Dominga presses her ear against the tree trunk.

"Now I'm sure I'm imagining things." It's Leonor. Her voice is muffled, but Dominga can tell she's somewhere near the birch trees. "I can't be seeing what I think I'm seeing."

"You can!" Lizeth says. "You are! It's a pastry picnic!"

"Did someone say pastries?" another voice chimes in. "Where?"

"Over here!" Leonor yells. "Under the birch trees!"

Dalia and Dominga turn to each other and silently squeal. But they don't dare come out of the tree trunk. Not yet. Not until the trap is sprung.

More footsteps thunder toward them.

"Are there any éclairs left?"

"Save some for me!"

"It sounds like the whole class!" Dominga whispers. Dalia blows the curls off her face. Behind them, her eyes glimmer.

Dalia and Dominga lean their heads together and hold their breath, waiting for the shrieks of surprise—screams of dismay!—that will tell them their plan has succeeded.

Instead they hear . . . nothing. The footsteps slow. The forest is silent except for the twittering of a few chatty birds.

"Perhaps they are so frightened they are . . . speechless?" Dominga suggests hopefully.

Then they hear the familiar sound of Profesora Colibrí's fan snap open. Dominga sits up, knocking her head against the tree trunk. "Uf!" she says, rubbing it.

"Princesas!" Profesora Colibrí shouts. "Who is responsible for this?"

Dalia grins. Dominga grins back. The time has come. They prepare to jump from the tree trunk and reveal themselves as the villains behind this wicked caper, terrible enough for the B.A.D.

But before they can, the soft thud of satin slippers comes skipping down the forest path. "Dalia and Dominga! It was them! *They* did this!"

Dominga can tell without seeing her that it's Inés. She can almost picture the fresh yellow gown.

"Whatever it is," Inés says. "*They're* the ones who did it, Profesora. No matter what they tell you."

This isn't how they planned to make their entrance, but it is as good an introduction as any. Dalia and Dominga pop out of the tree trunk.

"That's right!" Dalia announces.

"It was us!" Dominga declares.

No one boos.

No one hisses.

No one yells at them for ruining the whole day.

"Bravo!" Profesora Colibrí says, waving her fan. The rest of the princesas cheer.

"WHAT?!" demands Inés.

"Yeah," Dalia and Dominga say, confused. "What?" Then, as they look around the clearing, they slowly realize that somehow, everything has gone horribly, terribly, awfully *right*.

Dominga's stomach somersaults. Instead of desperate princesas fleeing a fire ant attack, she sees princesas sprawled on the grass, munching on pastries. Leonor dusts flakes of pastelito off her skirt, then licks a glob of cream cheese off her finger.

Lizeth alternates nibbles of éclair with bites of bizcochito. Everywhere Dominga looks, princesas are devouring a sweet feast while gentle sunlight spills through the birch leaves.

"What happened?" Dominga whispers. "Where are all the ants?"

She and Dalia turn toward the anthill. What they see is almost too horrible to believe. Princesas are escorting the fire ants home on rafts made of birch bark.

Dalia reaches into her thick hair and pulls. "WHY?"

"We're feeding them over here instead," Eloísa, an Emerald princesa, replies. "It's much safer, don't you think? If they eat with us, they might get squished, and *we* might get bitten."

That was the whole point. Dominga watches Eloísa gently set a raft of ants down at the base of the hill.

"Come back," Dominga pleads in her best attempt at ant-speak. But the insects ignore her.

Eloísa drops half an empanada into the hill, and the last of the ants scurry in after it.

Profesora Colibrí strides toward Dalia and Dominga, stopping to pick up an éclair on her way.

"Bravo," she congratulates them. "A picnic is exactly the refreshment we need to keep our minds sharp for the presentations. You thought of everyone's needs—the good of the whole ecosystem—and not just your own. What's more, you introduced the class to a most remarkable creature. Did you know that fire ants help loosen the soil to bring roots more oxygen? You are *true princesas*."

Dominga almost chokes.

Inés lifts up the edge of her spotless new gown to keep it from dragging in the dirt.

"Perdón, Profesora." She curtsies and stands

between Dalia and Dominga. Her red hair twisted into a neat braid, with her tiara sparkling on top. "Does this mean they *aren't* in any trouble?"

Profesora Colibrí chuckles behind her fan. "Trouble? Of course not. Dalia and Dominga have outdone themselves. Ten gems for Casita Opal and ten more for Casita Emerald."

The class cheers again.

Dalia shakes her head until a curtain of curls covers her face. Dominga wishes they could crawl back inside that tree trunk.

"In that case," Inés says, "you should know that *I* helped too. Ask Chef Luís-Esteban. They wouldn't be here if it weren't for me."

CHAPTER 18

Dalia and Dominga trudge to the farthest birch tree. They sink to the ground and slump side by side against its trunk.

"True princesas." Dominga repeats the terrible words. They leave a taste as bitter as black licorice in her mouth. She picks up an acorn and tosses it as far away as she can.

"She didn't have to say it in front of *everyone*," Dalia says.

Leonor crosses the clearing and stops in front of them. She holds out a bizcochito, partly crumbled.

"Thank you for bringing us the treats," she says. "And for keeping things interesting. I had a feeling you would. You two seem, I don't know, *different*."

"Tell that to Profesora Colibrí," Dominga mumbles.

"What was that?" Leonor asks.

"Nothing." Dominga takes the star-shaped cookie from Leonor. Cinnamon and sugar dust her fingers.

"Anyway, we're getting ready to start the presentations," Leonor continues, gesturing to the pond. "You can sit with me and Lizeth if you want. We could take turns keeping a lookout for Princesa Inés."

Dalia and Dominga glance at each other and

then at Leonor. She winks. "I'll save you a spot," she says.

Dalia watches her go. "Did you happen to notice," she asks, "the chocolate stains on Leonor's gloves?"

"Absolutely awful," Dominga says.

"She'll never get those out," Dalia adds.

"And she wasn't the only one."

They have the same terrible idea.

"Wrecking a royal wardrobe is at least somewhat sinister, don't you think?" Dalia asks.

"Dreadful even," Dominga agrees.

"Shall we alert the B.A.D.?"

Dominga takes her spell book from her pocket and tears out a page. She pulls the pencil from her hair and begins scribbling out the story of that morning's mayhem.

When the note is finished, Dalia rolls it up

tight. She loosens the laces of her boot and Don Ignacio slithers out.

Dalia taps his front claw in a rhythm that Dominga guesses is lizard-speak for "Deliver this, will you?"

Don Ignacio blinks. He flicks his tongue in and out.

"Thank you," Dalia says. She rips a thread from the bottom of her gown and uses it to fasten the note to Don Ignacio's collar. Once it's attached, he scurries away through the grass and dry leaves.

Dominga breaks the bizcochito in half and gives the bigger piece to Dalia.

She hears a flapping of wings above her and looks up in time to see the black-and-white hen leaping down from a low branch.

"I thought you were staying in the forest," Dominga clucks.

"I heard there was a picnic," the hen cackles back, landing on Dominga's shoulder. "I always wake up hungry from naps."

Dalia breaks off a piece of her bizcochito and feeds it to the hen.

"Just think," Dominga says between bites. "Tomorrow morning at breakfast, every princesa in the palace is going to bite into one of our jalapeño empanadas."

"I bet their eyes will water," Dalia says.

"And their palms will sweat!" Dominga shouts, leaping to her feet. The hen claws at her sleeve to keep from falling off.

"And their mouths will feel like they're about to breathe fire!"

Dominga can already imagine it.

TO: Dalia and Dominga

Princesas in Training,

Thank you for your letter. We enjoyed the visit from your clever lizard. The admissions council has met and determined that, unfortunately, you are not yet B.A.D. material. The picnic you planned was partially unpleasant, but only fairly dreadful. We invite you to try again.

Awfully sorry,
The B.A.D.

Acknowledgments

I am *dreadfully* grateful to Tiffany Colón, Abigail McAden, Melissa Schirmer, Maeve Norton, and the entire team at Scholastic; to Jennifer Laughran; to my parents, Sam and Lorraine Torres, for filling my head with stories; and as always, to David, Alice, and Soledad.

Read on for a sneak peek at Dalia and Dominga's next wicked plot:

BAD PRINCESSES 2:
MEET ME AT MIDNIGHT

They have been plotting all week. They must get there *after* the banquet tables have been set for dinner, but *before* the princesas arrive to eat. It is an awfully small slice of time.

But they have planned everything perfectly. The dining hall is deserted. Their boots thud dully on the gleaming checkerboard floor. Cloth napkins, in the colors of each Casita, are folded into rose shapes on the tables. Empty plates, soon to be filled with buttery empanadas and creamy egg custard, rest between gleaming gold forks and spoons. Paper banners with flowers cut into them flutter from the rafters, and lanterns filled with flickering candles fill the room with a soft, shimmering glow.

"Did you make the invitations?" Dominga asks, grabbing one of the two long window hooks that hang on the wall.

"Naturally," Dalia says, taking the other. "And our guests are frightfully pleased to join us. What about you? Are you prepared to spread the word?"

Dominga raises her hook and uses it to unlatch one of the high windows that line the hall. The window falls open a crack, and she moves on to the next one. "I've been practicing every night," she says.

Dalia hopes it is enough. Dominga is newer to animal speak than she is. She begins unhitching the windows on the opposite side of the room. They have only minutes now to finish their preparations with enough time to hurry back to the casitas and fall into the dinner line behind the unsuspecting princesas.

Dalia imagines what will happen after that. The princesas will sit down to eat as usual. Once everyone is settled and dishes are being passed, Dalia will give a signal—a squeak so thin and high-pitched the princesas won't notice it.

But the bats will.

They will swoop in through the open windows to feast on strawberries and melon and pineapple from one of Chef Luís-Esteban's fruit towers. The beating of hundreds of wings will snuff out all the candles.

Then, in the panicked darkness, Dominga will summon the rest of their guests. Rats. To scurry over satin-slippered toes. To wriggle under the linen tablecloths.

Dalia shivers in anticipation. The screams alone will secure their spots at the B.A.D. She is sure of it. Maybe the villains of the B.A.D. will be able to hear the terrified cries from their tower.

She opens the last window.

"The element of surprise is everything," she says. "We must get back to our casitas."